I0561289

Finding Love in Sweet Berry Cove

Ness Woodberry

Published by Lynda French, 2024.

Copyright © 2024 Ness Woodberry

All Rights Reserved

The characters and events portrayed in this book are fictitious. Any similarity to real persons, living or dead, is coincidental and not intended by the author.

No part of this book may be reproduced, or stored in a retrieval system, or transmitted in any form or by any means, electronic, mechanical, photocopying, recording, or otherwise, without express written permission: AuthorNessWoodberry@gmail.com

ISBN: 978-1-998074-35-8

Cover design by: Dezynetek

Publisher: Lynda French

Table of Contents

About this Book

For fans of heartwarming and emotional stories *"Finding Love in Sweet Berry Cove"*, a small-town romance suitable for all ages, is a captivating tale of love, friendship, and finding your place in the world.

Milly Clarke is excited to start her new job at the Young Family's Farm Shop. After years in foster care she longs to find a place to call home. Despite her natural shyness she is determined to meet people and make friends, but a small community isn't always welcoming to strangers.

Daniel Young has given up on love after being betrayed by his unfaithful girlfriend. He resents having Milly living in the farmhouse and rejects her attempts at friendship. But as they work side by side, he reluctantly discovers that there is much more to this young woman than meets the eye.

As Milly struggles to overcome the small town's reluctance to accept her, she forms friendships that give her the courage to fight for her happiness. But is it enough to overcome the challenges and obstacles when a nasty rumor threatens to tear her new life apart?

Dedication

To those who cherish their deep-down romantic side.

Once Upon A Time

Milly Clarke's new life feels like a fairy tale except right now it's turning into one of those darker stories from the Brothers Grimm.

She arrives at Young's Farm on a rainy night in the middle of August. After slogging through ankle-deep water from the sudden deluge Milly is relieved it's only a two-step climb to reach the wooden door.

This is roughly yanked open but with the light behind the figure all she can see is a huge ogre of a man whose height and width fill the doorway. Startled, she jerks back and it's only his quick reflex in grabbing her upper arm that prevents her tumbling down into the muddy water.

A deep, gravelly voice barks at her: "Who are you? What do you want?"

Flustered, Milly gulps loudly before stammering her reply: "I'm Milly Clarke, the new employee for the Young Family's Farm Shop."

He gives a grunting growl in response, *like a monster,* she thinks. Although the man's face is obscured by shadow she senses his disapproval bordering on dislike and amends that thought to *a very mean monster.*

Straightening her back Milly stretches to her full five feet, refusing to be cowed before she's even begun. "I would like to come in, please," she says and is happy to note she's spoken without a tremor in her voice.

Slowly, almost reluctantly, the big man steps back easily lifting the heavy suitcase out of her hand. "Where's your car? I don't see it."

"That's because I don't have one," she answers entering a traditional farmhouse kitchen. It's good to get out of the rain and into the welcoming comfort of the cozy room. Stepping into the light she can

1

see the man clearly and her eyes widen at his handsome face. *Well it would be handsome if he wasn't wearing that scowl,* she silently remarks.

"I came by taxi from the bus station."

"By taxi? I didn't hear a car pull up."

"No, the driver said he couldn't risk getting stuck in the mud so he dropped me by the gate."

"And left you to walk in this weather? in the dark? carrying this big case?" he angrily questions.

Milly doesn't answer, she's too surprised at his affronted tone.

"The driver was Gerry from the Sweet Berry Cove Cab Company, right? that's the only local firm." Talking more to himself than her the man continues: "It's owned by Henry Entwhistle but he can't see too well in the dark anymore so he hired a driver for the night shift. Yeah, it had to be Gerry."

Milly just shrugs. She neither knows nor cares who drove the cab, all she wants is to change out of her wet raincoat and sodden shoes.

At that moment an older woman comes hurrying in from the corridor introducing herself as Hannah Cairns, the housekeeper, and apologizing for missing Milly's arrival.

"Come inside and sit, dear. Let's get these wet things off and a hot drink in you," she declares. Milly finds the woman's no-nonsense manner reassuring.

Slipping out of her wet windbreaker and stepping out of soaked shoes she senses the man studying her. Looking up she catches him giving her the onceover. Meeting her gaze he sneers, obviously displeased with what he sees. After an initial pang at his disapproval Milly lifts her chin before turning her back on him and sitting down.

I know my clothes aren't new and fashionable but they are clean and presentable and that should be all that matters. This is a farm and I'm only here to work, she insists to herself.

She's traveled quite a distance all by herself to get to this unfamiliar place among strangers and the long day has taken its toll. Milly has to fight an urge to put her head down on the table and just cry it all out.

Maybe it's the quiver in Milly's lower lip or the stiffness of her shoulders but when Hannah Cairns sets down a steaming mug she gives the girl a friendly squeeze.

"You've met Daniel then, Daniel Young. He's the middle child," she adds, her statement full of meaning as she casts a sidelong look at the man. "Amos is the oldest, Daniel next, and Esther is the baby of the family even though she's sixteen-going-on-thirty."

Milly is grateful for Hannah's little joke and gives her a small smile. From the corner of her eye she notices Daniel leave without a word to either of them.

"Don't mind him, dear, that's just his way. Gruff and sullen on the outside but he's got a heart of gold underneath."

Milly is skeptical but she keeps her thoughts to herself.

Hannah hasn't sat down and now she tells Milly to bring her drink and they'll go to her room to get her settled. Looking around for her suitcase Hannah tells her Daniel will have taken it. This considerate action from a son of the house surprises Milly who thought he wouldn't help a mere worker.

Climbing the stairs they arrive at what Hannah calls *the bedroom floor* and go in the first door on their right.

"Now I know the job offer includes your own room but I hope that just for now you'll agree to share with Nora. As you can see there are two beds and it will only be for a couple of weeks. Nora and Amos are getting married on September 2nd and she's staying here until the wedding. I can find you another room but it's up another flight and not so comfortable being much smaller than this."

Milly hastens to assure Hannah that she doesn't mind in the least explaining: "I've never had a room of my own. I grew up in foster care, housed in a private home actually, so we all just squeezed in where we could."

Seeing Hannah's unhappy look she continues: "It's all I ever known and I was happy growing up there."

"Well my dear I certainly hope you'll find an even happier home here. Nora should be back in a half-hour or so but don't feel the need to wait up if you're tired. You've got a toilet through here and there's a shower and bathtub through the door directly across the hall. You'll be sharing it with Esther which isn't the happiest of circumstances but it's a farmhouse and we're lucky to have the facilities we've got."

Milly's suitcase is on one of the twin beds and she's annoyed to see it's already been opened. Hannah tsk-tsks about *wet leather on the bedspread* but slipping her hand between the bag and the cover mumbles *good, he dried it off first.*

Milly finds the thought of that man Daniel looking at her things, maybe even touching them, disconcerting. The packed clothes don't look like they've been disturbed, and she's pleased to see the topmost item is her fuzzy dressing-gown.

"Well my dear I don't live in so I will be heading to my home now unless you need anything else? Normally I work until 6:00, they eat an early supper at 5:00, and then I'm back at 10:00 next morning. But seeing it's your first day I'll be here at 7:00 to show you where everything is to get breakfast ready. You know it's part of your duties to cook the morning meal, right?"

"Oh yes," confirms Milly around a huge yawn. Hannah chuckles and tells the girl to get her sleepy-head to bed. She gives Milly's hand a quick squeeze before she leaves.

Milly follows that advice after a quick wash and change into her nightgown. When Nora Perez quietly enters soon after her room-mate is already sleeping soundly.

In A Land Far, Far Away

Population-wise Sweet Berry Cove could be a hamlet but because it has a Church (Calvary), School (K-8), Fire Department (volunteer), and a Public Library it qualifies as a rural village.

There are only a few hundred inhabitants, and the library is part of the school, so in truth it's really the Sweet Berry Cove Farmers' Cooperative – devoted to organic fruit farming – that puts the village on the map.

What began as a loosely knit group of concerned growers back in the 1930s and 40s developed into a powerful co-operative distributing under its renowned SBCFC brand.

Using Walter James's book *Look to the Land* as their starting point they established a chemical-free approach. The farmers were champions of the *sustainable agriculture movement* that expanded to embrace environmental protection in the 1960s and to this day. At least that's what it says on the co-op's website which Milly studied before traveling here.

The SBCFC promoted organic crops as its answer to preserving the family farm from takeover by huge commercial agribusinesses. What was lost in the bigger profits from a higher yield was gained in protection of their groundwater source and keeping their households intact.

Although some of the young people still move away from the land they've grown up on, the difference is they aren't forced to do so. After almost seventy-five years seven of the original eight families still farm in Sweet Berry Cove.

They lost one family just over twenty years ago when their soldier son was killed in the Middle East. The grieving parents bequeathed the farm to the co-op but of course the farmers insisted on paying them a fair price for the land.

One thing that distinguishes Sweet Berry Cove is that it's a dry village. In 1933 when Prohibition ended in the United States the farmers decreed no alcohol – not spirits, beer, or wine – could be sold or consumed. Under California's liquor laws that ban could be challenged but no one has ever been inclined to do so.

There are already many wine-growers in the region and rather than compete with those vineyards the co-op members only grow table grapes.

Armed with all this knowledge Milly looks forward to exploring her new home.

The farmland extends inland from the sheltered cove and ends at the ring of gently rising hills. Fruit thrives in the year-round temperate climate. The orchards contain all kinds of fruit-bearing trees and the fields are lush with berry bushes. The common land is grassy with a riot of wildflowers, perfect for the vitally important pollinators. The co-op employs its own bee keeper who has planted clover fields to ensure tasty honey packed with health benefits.

The rest of the residents are the professionals and business owners who cater to the needs of a farming community.

Like many places along the California coast the Main Street has a historically Spanish look. Flat roofs on mostly white - but also red, yellow, and pink - buildings with decorative edgings and arched windows on tree-lined streets made even prettier by huge planters of flowers. It's a small, attractive, gossipy place where people come together in fellowship and service.

A steep-sided escarpment drops down to the ocean although at the end of the horseshoe shape the ground flattens into a manageable scramble to a narrow beach. That area is owned by the village granting shore access to all residents. There's no pier or cabanas, but several sea kayaks are kept for communal use. The water here is safe with no rip-tides or currents. The scene is idyllic on this August morning.

Milly wakens a few minutes before the alarm she set on her phone goes off. Looking across at the other twin bed she sees a huddled form and is glad to get up without waking her room-mate at 6:00 am. The sun is already shining through the yellow curtains giving the room a bright glow. It doesn't take Milly an hour to shower, dress, and make her bed but she wants to be downstairs in good time for Hannah.

As she nears the kitchen Milly hears the sound of running water and hurries forward in dismay since the housekeeper has come in early especially for Milly's sake. Bursting through the door with an apology on her lips Milly is brought up short by the sight of Daniel Young dressed in running shorts and a t-shirt wet with sweat.

Startled, she blurts out: "What are you doing here?" and blushes furiously at her foolish question when he coldly informs her *I do live here, you know.*

Milly finds herself fervently hoping she doesn't have to work directly under this bad-tempered man.

Aloud she says: "Sorry! that was... oh... see I was expecting Hannah."

Although Milly's pretty face is a pleasant sight first thing in the morning Daniel can't help his brusque nature as he snaps: "At this hour?"

"She's coming in early to show me where everything is kept since I'll be making the breakfast each morning."

Daniel simply raises an eyebrow before draining the glass of water he's poured himself. He gets a refill and heads towards Milly who quickly steps out of his way. He continues marching past, facing forward, and she doesn't notice how his eyes cut sideways to take a good look at her morning-fresh face.

Moments later Hannah Cairns opens the back door and comes bustling in. It seems she's always hustling and hurrying, constantly on the move. She soon brings Milly up to speed on where everything is kept.

"The big fridge and both freezers are through here in the pantry along with most of the food, there's only a little kept in these cupboards. These dishes in the Welsh dresser are what we use for every day, cutlery and utensils are in those two drawers, and the hanging pots and pans are all you'll need for breakfast."

Milly follows Hannah as she hurries from one location to the other. All the supplies are stored logically and Milly is pleased to see that everything is within her short reach, although she has noted a sturdy two-step ladder in the corner. She's sure she'll be using that often!

"So, breakfast is cereal, fruit, danish, and a couple of hot items: eggs or pancakes with bacon or sausage or ham, or maybe serve just the meat with potatoes, whatever you like. In winter we do porridge as well.

This isn't a restaurant so the family will eat what you serve. Don't ask how they want their eggs cooked just make 'em the way you want: scrambled, poached, or fried. They know that if they want anything different they're welcome to make it themselves," Hannah states decisively.

"Well I'd like to make a good impression on my first day—"

"No," interrupts the housekeeper. "Begin as you mean to go on, I always say. If you treat them special today they'll expect it every day. So, how about scrambled eggs and bacon?"

Milly had been thinking pancakes made with fresh fruit but isn't going to argue. "Whatever you think, Hannah. I'll whip up a batch of biscuits, too."

"If you can make homemade biscuits you better make two batches. Actually make three since those boys must have hollow legs the way they eat."

"Umm, the boys? Daniel and–"

"No the twins, Micah and Joshua Young, cousins staying for the summer. They're always hungry! 11-year-olds who've been good for the most part but frankly I'll be glad to see them go back to their own home. Their parents are coming for Amos and Nora's wedding then the plan is the four of them will leave right after. You wouldn't credit how much those two kids can eat!"

"So how many will we have for breakfast?"

Counting it out on her fingers Hannah concludes: "Nine today, including us. That's Samuel, Amos, Nora, Daniel, Esther, and the twins. We eat in the dining-room. It means a few extra steps to carry dishes but believe me you'll be glad they're not in here getting underfoot, especially when they're in the mood to linger over their meal. Although Nora is a great help with the tidying up."

"Will she and Amos live here after they're married?"

"To begin with, for sure. There's been talk of them building a house for themselves but Samuel's also suggested maybe building him a cottage to move into instead. They'll probably still be discussing the merits of both plans in three or fours years from now. It's a farmhouse, lots of bedrooms and plenty of space for everyone." With a wink she adds: "Including a growing family when the time comes."

Hannah then pulls out a large tea trolley already loaded with a variety of cereal boxes. She adds two jugs of milk, sugar bowls, and butter dishes, then sends Milly to the pantry to find the maple syrup.

"Bring two jugs, we put one of each thing on either end of the table. I know we're not having pancakes but those boys like sweet syrup on everything. It will save you time in the morning if you set the table the night before with your serviettes, cutlery, condiments... you know. Then you only have to bring out the refrigerated stuff like orange juice and milk in the morning."

"Oh that is a good idea. I'm used to getting up early, that's not a problem, but I'm a bit of a dawdler. I like to take my time and hate rushing about."

"Ah, I'm pretty much the opposite. I want to get everything done as quick as I can then it's on to the next chore. My days just fly by!"

Milly smiles at the image of the older woman flying like a whirlwind through her housekeeping chores. Getting to work on her biscuits the two of them chat while they prepare the meal. Milly notes that the household uses real butter, unpasteurized honey, and whole milk. A huge basket of oranges and lemons sits beside a juicer so a supply of freshly squeezed juices are always available.

Once the food is ready it's carried into dining room on platters for the family to serve themselves.

"Don't worry about making too much, believe me there's no such thing as too much food while those twins are here. The schedule will change in the fall: the boys will be gone, Esther and Nora will be back in school, and the men will be in the orchards."

"Oh Nora goes to school?"

Hannah laughs loudly before explaining Nora is a teacher at the local school, teaching the grade five and six students. Esther catches a bus into town for the high-school.

"So breakfast is ready for... eight o'clock?"

"That's right. Most weekdays they won't linger over their meal so you should have time to eat and clear the table before you go to the shop at 9:30, ready to open up at 10:00. Just leave the dishes and I'll stack the dishwasher–"

"Oh I won't you with a mess to clean up," Milly assures the woman but Hannah shakes her head explaining *that's my job and I'm glad to have you here to get the first meal out of the way.*

"Nora's been doing it for the summer but she never learned how to cook so it's all been a bit hit-and-miss and pretty messy, too."

She shakes her head thinking back then briskly continues: "I cook a big lunch, it's really dinner because it's their main meal, for 1:00 and then a light meal like a bowl of soup or stew that I leave for them by 4:00 when I'm off."

Everyone arrives together and the table is noisy with their *good morning* greetings and exclamations over the hot biscuits. The fulsome compliments make Milly shy when she and Hannah sit down to eat. Introductions are made and Milly enjoys the camaraderie of a family breakfast.

Both Amos and Daniel get their good looks from their father and Amos has also inherited Samuel easy congenial manner. *Too bad that*

Daniel didn't take after his Dad and older brother in that respect, Milly thinks.

Nora is a pretty, vibrant, and friendly woman about half-a-dozen years older than Milly.

"No one is more thankful than I that you're here to take over the breakfast, Milly!" she exclaims in her musical voice. "I mean these people probably think they suffered plenty with my poor attempt at cooking but honestly it was traumatic trying to get everything coordinated!"

"I helped you, Nora," says Esther.

"When you woke up in time, you mean," replies Amos.

Before Esther can protest one twin exclaims: "The toast was always cold!"

"And soggy, too!" complains the other.

"Well there's nothing stopping you two from making your own meal if you don't like what's on your plate," states Hannah reasonably.

"Ugh, it wasn't that bad."

"No, we're just sayin'..."

Everyone tucks in and eats a good breakfast while maintaining a constant stream of chatter. Milly figures Nora's students must adore listening to her lovely voice teaching their lessons.

After the meal is over Milly has about half-an-hour for some preliminary exploring before going on to the Farm Shop.

Leaving the kitchen yard, still muddy from yesterday's wet, she follows a graveled path to the fields. From here she can see most of the farm's layout. Following the trail leads her around fields thick with berry bushes planted in neat rows. Rows and rows and rows.

I'm in a land far, far away, she thinks, *a world apart from the noisy urgency and pressure of city living where I've lived my whole life.*

It's a new and wonderful experience to savor the timelessness of the place. Sure, one hundred years ago that truck would have been a horse-drawn cart but the land with all its lush bounty growing green would have been here, quietly remaining the same.

It's like I've moved into another realm where time hasn't stood still, not with Nature's endless cycles of change, but where the very air is calming and peaceful. Where there's no place for drama, anxiety, or trauma. I feel like I've discovered the Garden of Eden, she marvels.

Milly has no idea how beautiful she looks standing in a field of sweet-smelling wildflowers with her youthful face turned up to absorb sunbeams. Enveloped in a shimmering glow with a light breeze teasing her hair... that's the sight greeting Daniel as he approaches from the path behind.

A twenty-year-old girl filled with the joy and goodness of this summer's day, her happiness brimming over to surround her as surely as the hum of the bees fills this field.

Turning in a lazy arc she catches sight of him and for a moment they freeze with their eyes locked, the beautiful girl and the handsome man. As his gaze intensifies a blush paints her cheeks until a hitch of breath breaks the spell. Acknowledging her with only a sharp nod Daniel turns his face away and quickly strides past.

Milly is briefly disappointed because the moment they shared seemed to hold such promise... but she's happy to hug the memory to herself knowing that Daniel's silence is so much better than a rebuff.

Wedding Bell Blues

With her usual animation Nora insists Milly is *a Godsend.*

"Truly, I can't tell you how relieved I am that you're such a fast learner. I've been fiddling with the demo web-store for ages and now you've got it up-and-running in three days! You're a marvel Milly, entering products and pricing and tax codes and shipping rates... I was getting awfully panicky because the wedding is happening in less than two weeks."

"Well you can relax, Nora. I've worked with this storefront a lot. Sunshine was really good about sending me for computer training and I'm familiar with quite a few software programs."

"So Milly, this woman Sunshine... surely that wasn't her real name, was it?"

"No, she re-christened herself from whatever she was originally called. She'd probably forgotten it herself. I've since learned her birth name but... it feels disrespectful to go against her wishes," with an earnest look on her face Milly says: "I really think our sense of self, our identities, matter, don't you?"

Satisfied with Nora's quick nod Milly continues: "She was *a true hippie chick,* as she put it, and she hung on to all the principles of peace and love and fellowship. Sunshine opened her home and her heart to me and I am forever grateful."

"Yes but... oh, never mind."

"No, go ahead. It doesn't matter what you say, it's not going to change my opinion of Sunshine, but if you've got questions then by all means go ahead and ask."

"Well, it was all kind of unofficial, right?"

"Kind of? No, it was totally 100 percent unofficial. Sunshine knew my grandmother through another unofficial charitable venture of hers modeled after *Meals on Wheels*—"

Nora interrupts to ask "Grandmother on your mother's side or...?"

"My mother's mother. I'm afraid I have no knowledge whatsoever about my father's family.

Anyhow, one day Sunshine dropped by with some frozen prepared meals for frail old Lizzie Sunderland and discovered me living there and running the elderly lady ragged.

Of course the whole story came out about my parents being killed in that car accident and as my only blood relative - she said - she feel duty-bound to raise her daughter's young child. But I was a very active kid and it was all too much for a woman pushing eighty."

"She was that old?"

"Yes, apparently my parents didn't marry until they were in their late thirties or early forties and I came along quite soon after, when my mother was forty-one or two. I'm not sure exactly how old Mom was when she had me. By time I was old enough to ask questions my grandmother had passed away."

"So your grandmother just... forgive me, I don't want to sound critical but it's just so... oh I don't know! Hard to believe, I guess."

"I suppose so... I mean I know how it looks and sounds and really you hear such awful things, don't you? but none of it seems odds to me because I was looked after so well.

Sunshine's offer to *take little Milly to her foster home,* which was really just a large family home, was gratefully accepted. I grew up alongside a variety of children of unknown antecedents in a casual but happy environment run by people who'd created their version of a perfect world.

There was no *aging out* rule to enforce so I was able to stay on after I turned sixteen. As Sunshine got older we had fewer children dropped off and eventually there were no more.

Sunshine paid for me to take computer training and that opened up a variety of possible careers. We were discussing the merits of different types of work and naturally Sunshine strongly favored the public sector being just as much against *fat cat capitalists* as she was anti-establishment.

Sunshine was a woman of strong opinions and although the world had moved on from what she acknowledged was *the starry-eyed idealism of the sixties* she remained true to her beliefs about equal rights for everyone."

"Wow, it's just hard to believe in this day-and-age, you know? I mean there's so much bureaucracy and red tape over every little thing... you wouldn't believe the hoops we have to make parents jump through at the school over surnames and who's got custody and who is authorized to pick students up. I know it's all for the protection of the children but we learn so much that truly isn't any of our business."

"I learned that my home was originally a commune. Back in the mid-sixties a group of like-minded people, *flower children,* bought up an area of land and settled into a peace-and-love lifestyle. Eventually they grew up. Some moved on to more conventional lives while others stayed but apparently the *free love* phase was over." She rolls her eyes and Nora giggles. "Still others, like our lawyer Matt Ellison, left and got educated and grew their businesses before returning to straddle both cultures."

"But what about money?"

"They didn't need much. The community strove to be as self-sufficient as possible and everyone worked at something. We had fishermen, farmers, trade workers. Those who worked from home - like the weavers and writers - looked after the kids and raised chickens."

Laughing she tells Nora: "They even tried having goats for the milk and to make cheese but it turned out those animals were just too mean. Sunshine used to have me in stitches with stories of embarrassing head-butts, and a whole batch of tie-dyed t-shirts drying in the sun got eaten – cotton t-shirts!"

"I've heard goats will eat anything but seriously? That's hilarious."

"Yeah, things like the t-shirts and other handicrafts were sold, or more commonly traded, at farmers markets. The barter system is alive and well with the self-employed and entrepreneurs."

"I still can't get over how easily the government just washed its hands of responsibility for you."

"I guess so long as there was no crime the authorities never bothered. We also had the Calvary church right from the very beginning apparently so that helped legitimize us. I suppose I just slipped through the cracks but from what I've heard..."

Milly shakes her head and her face turns sad. "Some of the kids who stayed with us told me stories about being in care with Child Protective Services and I think I was pretty lucky to escape that. I guess the government people were relieved to hand me off to a close relative and cross me off the books."

"So what ended up happening with Sunshine, she must have been getting on in years too?"

"After a couple of days of feeling rundown Sunshine suddenly asked me to call an ambulance for her. That was absolutely unheard-of. She died *enroute* to the hospital from a massive heart attack. It was such a shock, she'd never been seriously ill. Not ever."

"Oh that must have been devastating!" exclaims Nora with sympathy.

Nodding in agreement Milly takes a moment before composing herself to say: "It truly was but she died quickly and without a great deal of pain and I'm very thankful for that.

Although the panic and worry of that day, the day Sunshine died, was horrible it was only one day and one incident out of hundreds and hundreds and hundreds of wonderful days. I'm so grateful to have all these grand memories of happy, happy times in a loving home."

"I guess you're right that you were lucky because you've turned out to be a very nice, well-spoken young lady."

"Oh you!" laughs Milly, "You sound like an old lady yourself talking like that. Now, enough of this nonsense about me and let's finish deciding what foods will be offered for sale on the web-store."

About ten minutes earlier Esther had come into the farm shop and was rattling around impatiently. Both Milly and Nora turn to the girl with Nora asking what she's looking for.

"Oh nothing, I guess. I was just straightening up a little. What were you talking about anyway?"

"I was telling Milly how grateful I am that she's come to work here with us. Her knowledge is already proving to be a huge asset."

"I know everything there is to know about our Farm Shop," huffs Esther. "After all, it's got my family's name."

"Yes, but I'm talking about Milly's computer knowledge. She just zips through the software and it's so good to know that when I'm away the online store will be in capable hands."

Esther purses her lips in a pout before declaring she's quite certain she could learn it all too. Nora's voice takes on its soothing school-teacher tone as she assures her soon-to-be sister-in-law that that's true, but right now time - or rather the lack of - is the enemy.

Unfortunately Esther catches the raised-eyebrow-look Nora sends to Milly and isn't mollified at all.

"Oh just never mind. You don't want me in your wedding and now you don't want me in your stupid web-store. Well go ahead and keep your precious Milly because I don't want it anyhow."

Bursting into noisy tears Esther rushes out of the Farm Shop just as Janice Peart and Miz Tally are coming in. The older lady provides product on consignment and her neighbor helps her deliver it so the two of them are practically fixtures at the store.

"Whatever has upset Esther so much?" demands Janice Peart, her eyes sparkling at the prospect of insider gossip.

Nora ruefully wishes the new arrivals had been anybody but these two women. *Miz Tally is okay*, she amends in her mind, *but that Janice Peart of all people...*

Even Milly bites her lip in dismay but then, without thinking, she blurts out an answer using the title of an old song Sunshine loved to sing: "She's got *The Wedding Bell Blues*."

Chuckling at Milly's response Nora decides to make the best of a bad situation and just tell the nosy woman the truth. She knows Janice won't drop the subject.

"Esther is unhappy about not being a bridesmaid, but we're only having a very small wedding with Luisa as my maid-of-honor and Daniel as Amos's best man. Esther is too old to be a flower-girl and she can't be a bridesmaid without an usher."

"Yes I've been wondering why you are having such a small wedding party. I'm sure the two of you know plenty of people who'd happily stand up with you so why aren't you having more attendants?"

Biting back the urge to snap that *it's none of your business* Nora takes a deep breath and explains that she and Amos decided on a small, quiet wedding so an equally small wedding party works best.

The cool reserve in her tone would close the subject with anyone else but Janice isn't satisfied. "Hmm, but why don't you want a bigger wedding? What about your people? Don't they want to give you... oh! oh, is this all they can afford?"

"Janice!" reprimands Miz Tally. "That's none of our concern. Amos and Nora are old enough to know their own minds about what they want for their wedding. It is their special day to celebrate as they see fit."

"Oh, that's okay Miz Tally, everyone's going to know soon enough. There's just my father on my side and he'll be walking me down the aisle but then he has to immediately return back to his second family. He remarried after my mother died, but his new wife and my half-siblings aren't attending, so Dad won't be staying after the church ceremony is over."

Janice's mouth is working as she silently repeats all this over and over again, making sure she doesn't forget a single juicy tidbit. *And none of it made-up or speculation, all true and straight from the source!* she reminds herself triumphantly. Abandoning whatever purpose had originally brought her to the Farm Shop she hurries away to go spread the news.

Miz Tally simply tut-tuts at the departure of her next-door neighbor and pats Nora's hand saying it's very nice that her father has insisted on standing by his daughter on this special occasion. The old lady's kindness brings happy tears to Nora's eyes and Milly gives Miz Tally her sweetest smile.

Opening the shop door on to the sight of these happy women makes Daniel scowl as he demands to know what they did to make his little sister cry. Before anyone can explain Amos arrives as well wanting answers.

"Oh sweetheart it's my fault. I didn't realize how upset Esther would be over being left out of our wedding party, but I want Luisa with me." Nora's worried expression shows she regrets the hurt feelings, but she's determined to stick to her choice of her best friend as her attendant.

"Don't worry about it, hon. Esther's just a little spoiled and she figures since Daniel is included she should be as well."

Daniel isn't looking forward to the role he has to play as his brother's best man but he recognizes being chosen for the honor it is. If he himself ever marries, which he's adamant he won't, he'll be asking Amos to stand up for him.

"I guess I can see her point but... oh Amos, I really want my friend, not your sister."

Clearing her throat noisily Miz Tally gets their attention and after apologizing profusely for *poking my interfering nose in* asks "Can't Amos think of one other groomsman? Like maybe your good friend from the school, Peter Showalty the principal?"

"Oh!" both Amos and Nora exclaim looking at each other. "I never thought to ask," he says just as she puts in: "I'm sure he'd do it for us even if it is short notice and then we could include Esther as a bridesmaid.

Peter is such a good friend to both of us that it will be wonderful to have him be part of our wedding day. "

"It sure will, sweetheart. T

"Thank you, Miz Tally! That's an excellent idea."

The old lady beams at their praise.

"I wondered why you asked me instead of him in the first place," grumbles Daniel obviously not looking forward to hours of socializing and having to wear his good suit.

Ignoring the complaint in his brother's voice Amos states simply: "I forgot all about him. I mean you're the one I want at my side Dan, but I could have asked Peter as well. I know he'll jump at the chance because it will give him an excuse to get better acquainted with Milly."

All three women turn to him at that remark but their expressions are quite different: Nora is surprised, Miz Tally sparkles with interest, and Milly looks uncomfortable. Daniel frowns and Amos is blithely unaware of having dropped a minor bombshell.

It's decided that Amos will go see Peter right away. If he agrees to join them then Amos will send Nora a text so she can go ask Esther before the girl cries herself into a fit.

Eventually all the visitors go leaving Nora and Milly to get back to discussing the menu for the shop's online store.

"You only want to have one website and we've posted all the product at cash-and-carry pricing so now we need to separate the web-store items. My recommendation is only to ship long-life items like the preserves, juices, *et cetera*. That way you don't have to worry about a poor delivery service causing an unhappy customer."

"Oh that's a really good idea. I would hate to get a bad rating on one of those review sites all because of something beyond our control."

"Okay, so let's run through the whole menu and then sort what can be sold with delivery."

After much discussion over whether or not butter tarts had a long shelf-life and what a shame Miz Tally's fruit souffle can't be shipped despite her making it with Swiss meringue for stability, they settle on their menu.

The bulk of the Young Family's Farm Shop sales are for pies, cakes, fruit breads, pie filling, jams, jellies, syrups, dessert topping sauces, berry juices, lemonade, cider, butter tarts, muffins, canned and pickled berries. More than half of those goods can be sold online.

Dinner that night is a happy affair. Milly and Nora are satisfied with a good day's work in deciding the menu and entering the product into the web store app. Amos happily reports Peter's pleasure in being asked to stand with him at the ceremony, and Esther is exuberant at at being an attendant in the wedding party and demanding to go shopping in town for a proper bridesmaid dress.

The talk turns to other matters and Daniel, preferring to listen instead of joining the conversation, notices his sister casting puzzled but slightly resentful glances at Milly. He's surprised because she's never shown any jealousy over Nora's presence. Turning the matter over in his mind he decides it must be the evident friendship between the two women that's causing Esther's envy.

Catching her unguarded look of yearning at the women's easy camaraderie he understands why being a member of the wedding party is so important to his sister.

For such a quiet and apparently unassuming person Milly Clarke somehow does make her presence felt.

The Wicked Stepmother

The old farmhouse has plenty of windows allowing cool breezes to blow through at night. Sitting propped up by pillows in her bed Milly pulls the cover, a handmade quilt, to her waist. When she settles down to sleep she'll have it tucked under her chin knowing she'll need the warmth by time the wee hours roll round.

She and Nora are talking about the plans that have been made for the wedding.

"I am sorry to hear you won't have family there to wish you well but if I ever marry–"

"Oh I'm sure you will," cuts in Nora. She's sitting at the vanity using make-up remover pads to wipe off her mascara.

"Well I do hope to, some day," agrees Milly before continuing: "but when I do I won't have a single relative there. At least you'll have your Dad at the church."

Nora turns to face Milly with her brow creased into a worried look.

"I was figuring that he'll come and do his duty by me but once I'm married Dad will basically wash his hands of me. I don't like the idea but I've come to terms with it and I'll have Amos by my side as support. But now I've started wondering if Dad's going to be a no-show at the last minute."

"Why would you even think that? Is he... is your father um... " Milly pauses searching for an acceptable word for the type of person Sunshine used to call *a mushy-brain*. "uh, unreliable for some reason?"

"Oh you mean like an addict or an alcoholic? Oh no, thank goodness, no! I'm worried because of his wife.

Teresita is unbelievably jealous and not just about me reminding him he had another wife before her even though she's passed away. No, she's jealous of the teller at the bank, of the cashier in the grocery store, of the server at the fast-food take-out window... of anyone who catches Dad's attention even for the few minutes it takes to complete a business transaction. Jealousy like that is a horrible, horrible thing."

"Has he... forgive me speaking bluntly Nora, but has your father given her reason to think that way?"

"Oh no, not at all. Dad's loyal to his marriage. Plus it's not just women she's jealous of. No, Teresita's jealousy is hinged on her, and only her, being the center of her family's universe.

I remember one time Dad was late coming home from work, only by an hour, but she had driven herself into hysterics in that time. First she was all anger about him drinking in the bar with his men friends. Then, practically foaming at the mouth, she started shouting about him meeting up with another woman. Next she was certain he'd been killed in a car accident and began shrieking and sobbing, it was quite a frightening display.

And poor Dad, it turns out he'd had a flat tire and his new car didn't include a spare! Can you imagine that? it never occurred to him to ever look until he needed to and then... anyhow, after dealing with that schemozzle he sure didn't need a crazy lady screaming at him but... he doesn't complain.

When I still lived near them and visited from time to time I witnessed her appalling behavior. She's even jealous of anyone who interacts with her kids. Their teachers, the woman who drives the school-bus, the old librarian... it's sad but her children have learned never to even compliment or smile at anyone or their mother will accuse them of no longer loving her.

Teresita is convinced that the affection that is hers by right is constantly at risk of being stolen away."

"I've never seen or heard of anyone behaving like that," says Milly giving her head a shake.

"It's awful. Teresita howls and hyperventilates until she collapses in a panic attack. Dad has never given her the slightest cause, he's 100 percent faithful and always has been, but she hates his dead wife who he had a child with so she hates me. She's turned into the wicked stepmother."

"Oh, I'm so sorry to hear this. What a burden for your poor father, and such an ordeal for her children. What on earth will happen when they grow up and want to date and marry?"

"I'm sure she'll drive them away. They'll probably escape by going to college out-of-state and that will make her positively ill. No, I'm afraid that all of Teresita's fears will come true and it will be down to her own behavior, a self-fulfilling prophecy kind of thing."

"I know she's done her best to make you miserable Nora, but with what you've told me I can't help feeling sorry for the woman. Was she always this way or did she have some bad experience?"

"I wondered about that, too. I mean my father is not a stupid man and I couldn't understand why he let himself get trapped this way, why he didn't see through her. But I've since seen her in action and she just steamrollers over all objections. She's so intense and hyper and shrill it's simply easier to give in.

Plus she caught him on the rebound, way too soon after my mother's death, and after less than a week she had him off on a Vegas weekend and came home married."

"Oh no. It does sound like she's a bit of a schemer who took advantage."

"Totally but Dad is also to blame for ignoring the red flags and just falling for what he could see. Did I mention that Teresita is drop-dead gorgeous? She's really stunning with a beautiful face and figure, but she's classy and elegant with it. She's the type other women are jealous of.

I don't know if there was a serious heartbreak in her past, or if she grew up with all kinds of insecurities, I don't know. But I believe her jealousy is bad enough to be called a sickness, and honestly? I'll be hurt but not terribly shocked if Dad bails on me at the last minute."

"I have no recollection of my parents but if they'd lived I think I would have expected more from them then this treatment you're getting. Jealousy is a truly terrible, bitter thing.

However, rotten as this is you can't control other people's actions so what's your contingency plan just in case?"

"I don't have one. I haven't even liked thinking about the possibility because it really will hurt me but you're right. It sounds like a mean thing to say but I bet Teresita is already plotting how to keep Dad away. So, I guess I should consider..."

"Samuel will do it. Tomorrow we'll talk to him and then give Reverend Smithson a heads-up that if you're being escorted down the aisle on Samuel's arm that he needs to drop that phrase about *who gives this woman away* or however it's worded."

Nora hurries across the room and embraces Milly in a heartfelt hug saying: "Thank you Milly, thanks! Your clear-headed sensible solution has calmed me down. I was letting these *what if* worries muddle my brain. Really I feel so much better now that there's a fallback solution. Okay, good."

"I'm very glad I can help you cross a worry off your list!" Milly giggles, then sobering adds: "Those *what if* worries are the worst because you can't stop yourself even though you know you must."

"Oh I know exactly what you mean," confirms Nora getting up from where she'd been sitting at the side of the bed and heading into their *ensuite* restroom to wash her face before applying nighttime moisturizer.

Milly, luckily blessed with a clear complexion, has no pampering routine so she slides down in her bed and settles herself to sleep.

A Dream Come True

The family is gathered round the table to enjoy a leisurely mid-day meal.

Sunday mornings are always a scramble so breakfast ends up being a hit or miss affair for most of them. Milly prepares the food but with the whole family trying to get ready for church – after sleeping in as long as possible! – few of them find the time to sit down and eat. Instead it's a hustle to get to the service on time.

Hannah Cairns comes in to cook and serve a hot meal on Sundays and in turn works just a half-day on Wednesdays. Hannah isn't a churchgoer herself but she's always keen to hear the news that the family members bring home from the congregation.

In a small community talk really does travel quickly, and even the most trivial items are interesting when they involve your neighbors. In the past Hannah has been frustrated when she hears a bit of gossip days later because the Young menfolk couldn't be bothered to pass it on.

Today, though, she is regaled with stories and almost all of them revolve around Milly. First Hannah asks about the banns being read and yes, that happened for the second week.

"I had heard of that but didn't know it still happened, I thought it was just an old-time thing from books," comments Milly with a smile.

"Well you don't have to have them read, and I guess lots of churches no longer do, but our Calvary Church does."

"That's because Stephen enjoys it so much. He assures me he's always starts out very solemn but ends up grinning away because he loves weddings," chuckles Samuel. Reverend Smithson is his closest friend although Samuel, raised Catholic, never attends any services.

"He's a very friendly, pleasant man," agrees Milly.

"Well I guess you'd think that since he sure stood in the doorway for ages talking to you," complains one of the twins.

"Yeah, you really held up the line forever, Milly," adds the other.

"It certainly wasn't Milly's fault. It was Reverend Smithson who was doing all the talking," says Nora coming to Milly's defense.

"He just thanked me for attending, same as he did with everyone else."

Amos laughs loudly saying: "Oh hardly! He talked to you for so long old Jacky Paulson started shoving into me and muttering about a bottleneck and *keeping a man from his dinner.*"

Esther has a complaint of her own claiming: "That Mr. Paulson put his walker right down on my foot and didn't even apologize when I cried out. My toes still hurt."

"I bet he follows the old policy of not eating before church which makes him even more grumpy and cantankerous than he usually is," says Samuel, still chuckling. He's in a happy mood himself this morning.

"Oh but Hannah the real excitement came after we all finally got through the goodbyes and out the door only to discover a man was waiting to see Milly."

Hannah's eyes fly between Nora and Milly demanding to know *what man? who was it?*

"It was that cab driver, Gerry something-or-other, and he's just standing there until he spots Milly coming out and then he pulls off his cap and steps forward *to apologize*! He was saying he was sorry for making her walk all the way from the gate in the bad weather and he should have brought her safely to our door."

"Well that's certainly true–" asserts Hannah but then one of the twins interrupts shouting: "You should have seen the shiner he had!"

"Wha–? You mean he had a black eye?"

Both twins nod with gleeful enthusiasm. One begins: "The biggest black eye ever and–"

"A bandage over the top of his nose as well," concludes the other.

Amos confirms that "Somebody laid a beating on Gerry and I'm guessing this apology was to prevent him getting another licking." He casts a sidelong look at his brother but Daniel is concentrating on cutting the food on his plate.

Milly, from her seat beside Daniel could have looked up at him and seen his faint smirk but she isn't paying him any attention. Instead she speaks in a worried tone of voice saying she is sure there's no connection. The older family members are all careful to avoid catching Daniel's eye.

Soon afterwards Hannah starts stacking the plates and both Milly and Nora get up to help her clear the table.

"Nora you haven't told me much about your honeymoon. I know sometimes that's a secret but you did mention a cruise and that you'd be gone for over a month was it?"

Her face shining Nora warns Milly that she is about to get her ears talked off with the story of the much-anticipated honeymoon trip.

Slouching her way into the kitchen Esther moans: "Oh we're not going to talk about this cruise *again,* are we?"

"You don't have to talk at all, Esther. Just politely listen... like Milly is."

"Hey! it's not politeness, I'm really interested, I want to hear all about it. This trip I made to Sweet Berry Cove is the longest distance I've ever traveled. Well, I guess coming from San Diego to my grandmother's was more but since I was only a toddler I have no memory of that at all."

"I'd like to go to San Diego and visit the Zoo, it's very famous," announces Esther. The two older women smile and nod at her but when there's nothing more said they return to their conversation.

"So the cruise is almost two months long. We go off on September 4th, the Monday, and don't get back here until October 27th."

"Oh wow!" exclaims Milly, wide-eyed. "That's a long trip."

"It's a long time to be away from the farm. We're busy year-round but a little less busy now and both Samuel and Daniel will cover Amos's absence here and with the consortium. Samuel, of course, knows all the ins and outs of the day-to-day operation already and Daniel needs to learn it anyhow. He'll probably end up taking over that job some day."

"Really? he doesn't strike me as... oh! I shouldn't say anything I really don't know him at all–"

"Let me guess, you were about to say Daniel doesn't seem like a people person, right?" Nora laughs when Milly gives a shamefaced nod. "Well you're right, he's not, but because he is the quiet, listening type when he does say something people pay attention. Daniel is a well-educated, articulate man. He's full of surprises."

Milly doesn't want to show too much interest, she doesn't want to seem nosy and prying. She returns to the subject of the honeymoon.

"So the wedding is Saturday the 2nd and then will you stay here that night?"

With a pretty blush Nora gushes about Amos booking a honeymoon suite at a fancy boutique hotel in Los Angeles for the Saturday and Sunday nights since the ship sails from that city.

"We're cruising on the Princess line to Australia and New Zealand with stops at a bunch of different islands along the way including Hawaii, Tahiti, Fiji, and Samoa."

Milly's mouth has dropped open in wonder. "I've heard of all those places and oh my, what an adventure! It must be awfully expensive."

"Well it's off-season rates because the kids are back in school but even so we were both surprised at how reasonable it is. $17,000 for the two of us and that includes all fees and taxes."

Milly's eyes are huge as she slowly sounds out the words *seventeen thousand dollars!* in a shocked tone.

"Yeah I guess it does sound like a lot but Milly just think how much we would spend for... let's see it's um... 57? yeah 57 nights in resort hotels? Plus, all our meals are included so the only extra expenses will be for any shopping we do at the ports of call."

"You have to buy souvenirs!" insists Esther. Nora rolls her eyes at the teen confirming that they will definitely be bringing back presents.

Milly's mind is still wrapped up in how casually Nora weighs the costs of hotels versus cruises and being all logical and reasonable about it. It's a new way of thinking that's incredibly foreign to Milly.

Sunshine turned her back on her wealthy family to live the hippie lifestyle. The inhabitants of her commune shunned the almighty dollar preferring handcrafted goods and homegrown food. And, when necessary, bartering their goods and services with like-minded friends.

She never wanted to discuss the income regularly deposited into the bank and told Milly just to pay and then forget the bills because money wasn't something worth bothering about. Milly never questioned Sunshine's orders.

Milly brings her thoughts back to the present and tunes in to the conversation just as Nora teases Esther saying: "How about a grass skirt from Polynesia?"

Frowning Esther replies doubtfully: "I don't think I'd get much wear out of that... maybe for a costume party at Halloween."

Nora reaches over to give the girl a quick hug and tells her: "I'm just kidding."

"Oh good, because I'd really rather have South Sea pearls."

Milly gasps but Nora just laughs.

"Well I think it sounds absolutely wonderful. A dream come true!"

Turning serious Nora agrees explaining that farming life doesn't allow for frequent holidays which makes this vacation extra-special. "It's a once-in-a-lifetime trip and it will give us a lifetime's worth of memories. I feel so blessed."

"I'm so happy for you, Nora. For you and Amos both."

The farm shop isn't open on Sundays at this time of year. The tourist season is Spring and early Summer, and the locals do their shopping on weekdays. But Esther wanders over there, happy to escape wedding talk and kitchen chores.

She knows one or both of her brothers will be unloading boxes into the shop's storage area. Everything is being stored in anticipation of great things coming from this online store.

Esther swings her legs on the stool. She's been watching her brothers at work and now she's feeling slightly bored. Although the girl would never admit it she's more than ready to go back to school in a couple of weeks. She finds herself drifting into the farm shop more and more, slipping behind the counter – not to work, but to claim the stool – listening to the conversations going on around her.

Today it's *that Janice Peart*, as the woman is always referred to, and Miz Tally who have come into the shop as one of their many stops on their roundabout way home from Church.

"Reverend Smithson made quite a show of greeting Milly after the service, did you notice?"

"Of course I did! When he shook her hand I thought he was never going to let go, it was so sweet," says Miz Tally agreeably.

"Sweet? I don't know about that, but I do know that she didn't pull away none too soon either," adds Janice with a decisive nod.

Miz Tally's eyes light up as she exclaims: "Oh I wonder... do you think she might be interested in him? We already know that he's interested in her."

That bit of gossip makes Esther sit up stating: "Eww, he's so old. He's like my Dad's age, you know".

"Esther! your father isn't an old man by any means. He keeps himself fit and is actively involved in the community. Although he passed on the day-to-day operations of the co-op to Amos he's still active in the administration and the marketing of the brand."

"Well yeah, I know all that, but he doesn't like um... date or anything, and he doesn't want to!"

That's when Janice Peart pipes up and says "So what if he does? Your father isn't elderly, he could still find happiness with a new wife."

"But not Milly!" squeals the teenager.

Miz Tally gives what she imagines is a reassuring nod telling Esther that May-December romances often make very successful marriages.

"Oh my dear, he's at the age where he's extremely likely to be looking for companionship."

"He's got me and my brothers, he doesn't need anyone else."

Miz Tally pauses to think over her reply. It's obvious from their scowls that both Esther and Janice hate the idea of Samuel and Milly marrying. She hopes to make her point while softening the sharp sarcasm Janice is sure to provide.

"Esther, while your father isn't old he's at that turning-point in his life when he realizes he has more of a past than a future. I'm sure you've heard of men having a mid-life crises, right?"

"Yeah but they just go out and buy a sports car," the girl says.

Laughing Miz Tally agrees that *yes, some do* then continues saying: "But others take stock of what they want going forward and very, very often that involves finding a romantic partner."

Esther sputters in her haste to answer: "No! if he wanted a girlfriend he's have found somebody local by now–"

But Miz Tally interrupts her explaining: "Ah, but that's the catch, dear. He's known all the local ladies for most of their lives and while he's full of goodwill and friendship towards them that's all it is.

Esther, the very first time Samuel Young visited Sweet Berry Cove and saw your mother he fell head over heels in love with her. They were only teenagers but it was true love all right. No one was surprised when they married as soon as he finished his schooling.

I remember Samuel back then and he was a fine-looking man with good prospects who could have his pick of the girls in his age group but he never had eyes for anyone else."

"But.." Esther isn't happy with the direction the conversation has taken. Suddenly she blurts out: "I thought we were talking about the Reverend, not Dad."

"Oh we are. It's Reverend Smithson who is showing feelings for Milly, not your father. That doesn't mean she isn't angling for him too though," puts in Janice with a sour expression.

Miz Tally recalls how Janice was one of the young women in Samuel and Ruth's circle who was always making eyes at him.

Determined to move off the distressing subject Miz Tally asks if there will be a 50th birthday celebration for the Rev. As she rightly guessed Janice perks up at the suggestion.

"Oh that's an excellent idea. You know Esther, your father refused to let us do a thing last year to honor his 50th. I don't know why he cares that we know how old he is – it's not like it's a secret!"

Miz Tally remarks: "Oh I don't think it's vanity, dear. He's just one of those low-key men who don't like a fuss."

When the women leave Esther heads off as well, moodily kicking at stones on her way back to the farmhouse.

Hannah Cairns, just leaving to go to her own home, sees the girl coming into the kitchen yard and demands to know why Esther has *a face like a wet weekend.*

"Oh! that's a funny saying, I've never heard it before."

"Well I've never seen you looking like this before. What's wrong, honey?"

"Do you think May-December marriages are a good thing?"

"Huh! Now what's got you thinking about that, hmm?"

"Oh just something Miz Tally was sayin' to that Janice Peart."

"Those two gossips! Well, there's no harm in Miz Tally but that Janice can be pure poison. Anyhow, offhand I can't think of anyone I know in a May-December marriage but I'm well aware that men of a certain age do do funny things. Hmm, I wonder who the old biddies meant?"

"They started out talking about the Reverend and Milly and then for some reason they switched to Dad."

"Ah, I see. Well Esther your father isn't making eyes at anybody so far as I can tell so I wouldn't be worrying about it. On the other hand, I'm sure you want your Dad to be happy so if he ever did meet someone well then, that would be good for him after being alone all these years, right?"

With a dissatisfied sigh and a scowl Esther mumbles in reply: "I s'pose."

My Hero

Back in the farmhouse Nora exclaims with a light laugh: "Milly! I can't believe it but we've been chattering away for over an hour. You're just so easy to talk to."

Nora's compliment makes Milly smile so hard her cheeks hurt. "I was thinking the same thing when we were talking before bed the other night. I feel like I've known you for the longest time!"

This connection, this camaraderie, is exactly what I've always wanted, she thinks to herself. *It's exactly what I've been hoping to find.*

While riding the Greyhound to her new home she made a promise to herself, resolving to make a real effort to fight against her natural shyness. *I have to open up and be a friendly person myself if I want to make friends. It's going to be hard but I'm determined to make this work, I've been living a solitary life for too long.*

The two women have been tidying up the display of wedding presents dropped off at the farmhouse over the past week. Everyone who comes by is invited to place their gift in the front room and naturally they want to see what's already been delivered and by whom.

Most take the chance to sneak a look at labels and makers' imprints, too. So Milly and Nora are making sure the cards match the presents, and polishing off any messy fingerprints.

Naturally everyone who comes by is offered a hot or cold drink with a slice of pie or cake.

While working they've talked about the wedding and living in Sweet Berry Cove.

"I've wandered all around the orchards and berry fields of the farm but I haven't really explored the village yet. I have managed to meet a lot of people through the shop, and at church, too."

"Oh I'm quite sure just about everybody's come by the shop to get a look at you. Let's hope the busybodies at least had the courtesy to make a purchase while they were poking their noses into your business!" declares Nora with a mock-stern expression.

Milly giggles and confirms that Amos said the takings had definitely increased since she started work. "People did ask questions about me but they weren't very forthcoming about themselves. I can't really say I got to know anyone..."

As Milly's voice trails off Nora nods knowingly. "It is an insular place, which I guess is only to be expected when you're fairly isolated and pretty much self-sufficient. Most of the residents were born here. A lot of them moved away for jobs or marriages but they returned to retire or when their circumstances changed. They call it *God's country* and I think they're right. But I didn't always think that way."

Nora pauses in her tidying up to sit down. Gesturing for Milly to join her on the love-seat she takes hold of the younger woman's hands before continuing:

"Milly, your lack of family will be held against you here but you're young and pretty and white and though I know that isn't the politically correct thing to say it is true. Those things are going to help you break through eventually.

I was not welcome when I first came and neither was Luisa because we're Latina and there's a long history of conflict over territories, jobs, religion, you name it. I found a champion in my boss, Peter Showalty, when he witnessed some snubs and prejudice directed my way.

He's such a sweet man it never occurred to him that people might object to him hiring a teacher called Eleanora Perez. He was so angry at them and so apologetic to me."

"Oh Nora, that's really awful. Come to think of it though, from what I've seen this place is what Sunshine would have called *a real whitebread community.*"

"And she would have been right on the money. I mean, no one actually called me *a poor Mexican* to my face, but based on their sneers it sure was in their thoughts. Peter Showalty got ahead of any complaints by calling them out on their narrowmindedness. By putting everyone on the defensive he basically shamed them into at least giving me chance to prove myself and it really wasn't long before they accepted me.

My close friend Luisa didn't have anyone like Peter on her side since she's a self-employed professional but this community had no vet so it grudgingly decided she was better than nothing.

Luisa's not the type to back down or feel the need to prove herself. She's prickly with her friends never mind anyone who crosses her! There were conflicts, but I think she earned respect by standing up for herself and, of course, being extremely good at her job. She was kind enough to take me *under her wing* when I arrived here."

"I'll meet her at the wedding or the morning of, I suppose. As your maid-of-honor she'll be here to help you get ready."

"That's right, Luisa will arrive bright and early. She's a few years older than me and I'm a few years older than you but I just know you two are going to hit if off. Luisa is a very warm person and she's been a really good friend to me.

At one time I wondered if she and Peter might not make a go of it but they've never been more than friendly and Luisa seems quite content as a single woman. She's very serious about her career and spent years training so the clinic is pretty much her whole life. For now, anyways.

You know it wasn't until I started dating Amos that I felt I'd finally been accepted as a Sweet Berry Cove inhabitant."

"Now that does surprise me. I would have guessed possible resentment or jealousy at an outsider snapping up a catch like Amos Young. Oh! I don't mean to sound facetious, I think Amos is great. Anyone from the founding farm families will be sought-after."

"You know I never really thought about it that way. Probably because he didn't give me a chance to wonder what anyone else thought. Amos was very persistent and told me afterwards that he'd been ready to propose one week in but figured I'd think he was crazy, and yeah, that's exactly what I would have thought!

Amos said he just knew right away that I was the one for him so he then proceeded to monopolize all my time and attention until I couldn't imagine a life without him in it.

But stepping back to see how our whirlwind courtship might look to others... hmm, I guess Amos *legitimized* me in their eyes."

"Well I've only been here a few days and his love for you is so obvious. Whenever you're in the room he's always looking at you, and if you're not in the room he's got his eyes on the door waiting for you to appear."

"Oh Milly, that's such a lovely to say!" Nora's eyes shine with emotion as she tightens her grip to squeeze Milly's hand. "I'm so glad you're here."

"I really like being here at the farm, and it's been great working with you in the shop, Nora."

"Well, Amos and I can enjoy our honeymoon without worrying since both the farm and the Farm Shop are in capable hands. I just wish you could have hit it off better with Daniel, but I know he's a difficult guy."

"I'm willing to be friends with him but... well I don't know him at all but it seems like he wants nothing to do with me."

"Oh, it's not you personally Milly, it's all women. It's because of... oh heck I don't like talking behind his back. I can't, Daniel is my second favorite man in the whole world."

"Daniel is?!" Milly doesn't even bother to hide her surprise at Nora's remark.

"Ha, you're shocked but I have good reason and I can definitely share that story, I tell it to everyone who will listen!"

"Oh now you've got me on the edge of my seat!"

"Well, it's only a matter of Daniel saving Amos's life, you know. Daniel will always be my hero."

"Oh my, whatever happened?"

Nora glances at her watch saying: "Good, we've got plenty of time, it's not a long story but I have to give you a bit of background first.

Samuel tried branching out into dairy farming but it was too much effort for too little return. Dairy is a very competitive market, the cows need a lot of pasture to graze, and then there's the milking and the barns and the hay... it just wasn't a money-maker. Luckily he's not a stubborn man and when he saw that it wasn't working he shut it down.

The livestock and equipment were easy to sell but he got stuck with George, the bull. The farmer who bought the cows didn't want him.

45

So, George has been up for sale for ages but no one's been interested in buying him."

"Do people eat bulls? or I guess I should say bull meat? I grew up with a lot of vegetarians and vegans so we didn't have a lot of meat meals and when we did it was usually chicken."

"Bull as beef isn't popular. I've never eaten it myself but Amos tells me it's a gamy meat that's tougher than cattle beef. Since bulls are muscular animals the meat is lean which is probably healthier but less fat means it's dry."

"Oh, I've heard that about buffalo meat, too."

"Yeah, so nasty old George doesn't have to worry about going to the butchers. Luisa said George is a particularly bad-tempered bull which makes him difficult to handle and that doesn't help. They'll never be able to sell him.

Anyhow, I hate the monster because he almost killed Amos and would have if not for Daniel's quick intervention."

"Oh no, what happened?"

"Have you heard of that sport of *running with the bulls* in Spain?"

"Yes, we heard it on the radio not that long ago. I think they only aired the item because someone got hurt and that made it newsworthy."

"I'm not surprised. Bulls run much faster than humans can so I'm sure lots of people get hurt. I can't imagine anyone wanting to do something crazy like that but it takes all sorts."

"Thrill-seekers, I guess?"

"Yeah, but they prefer to call themselves *adrenaline-junkies*."

Milly laughs asking: "Is that supposed to sound better?"

"Oh I know. Anyhow, on this particular day Amos was meeting up with Daniel to mend a fence and he took a foolish risk by deciding to cut across George's field since the bull was grazing at the opposite end. Maybe he would have gotten across safely but George spotted him. Amos said once he realized George was watching he panicked and made the mistake of running."

"Well of course he would run!" Milly said breathlessly, totally caught up in the tale.

"That's what I said! but apparently running is the worst thing to do because it encourages the bull to charge. Amos was so busy looking over his shoulder he tripped and fell, hurting his ankle.

Daniel grabbed a fence rail and jumped into the field because he's a real hero who risked his life without a moment's hesitation. He pulled off his shirt and waved it around to distract George–"

Milly interrupts asking: "Was it a red shirt?"

"No, apparently that thing about bulls hating the color red is just a myth because they're color-blind. Matadors do wave a red cape but it's the flapping cloth that angers the bull, not the fact that it's red.

Anyhow Daniel dodged and turned and ran in circles until Amos could drag himself up and over the fence. By time he got to safety his sore ankle was now a bad sprain."

"What about Daniel?"

"Turns out he did have to hit George on the nose with the fence rail he was smart enough to bring. The bull backed off long enough for Daniel to vault over the fence as well. Neither of the men know exactly how long all of this took but Amos figures probably less than ten minutes."

"That doesn't seem long but I guess it is when you're trapped with an angry bull. I mean, they're big animals, aren't they?"

"Oh yes! Luisa told me the average bull weighs about 1800 pounds and that George is bigger than most. He won't live much longer, he's twenty now, and he's lucky he'll die of old age. Most livestock doesn't. Of course if it was up to me he'd have been ground into dog food!"

"Oh Nora! You can't blame the bull."

"Huh, who says I can't?"

A Rose By Any Other Name

"Sandy can I have another pancake? asks Joshua.

"Me too, Sandy and bring more butter," chimes in his twin. "Oh yeah, and more syrup, Sandy."

"Say *please Sandy*," admonishes Esther, giggling.

"Yeah Micah, say *please* to Sandy," Joshua echoes, kicking his brother's chair.

"Right! Sorry Sandy, can you *please* bring us more syrup."

The two boys snicker together, looking at their cousin for approval. She joins them in the joke. Samuel has been looking back and forth between his nephews with a confused expression.

He finally puts down his knife and fork saying: "I do apologize for my mistake in calling you Milly, Sandy–" but before he can finish the three youngest at the table collapse into howls of laughter.

"Be quiet!" thunders Daniel in a growl.

Everyone goes silent and in his usual mild voice Samuel thanks his second son before continuing: "I'm sorry, but I thought your name was Milly."

Looking Samuel in the eye Milly calmly replies, "It is Milly."

Samuel frowns saying: "But the children call you Sandy?" turning his statement into a question.

"Oh Daddy," interrupts Esther, sounding exasperated. "Her name is Melisandre. So her nickname should be Melly not Milly! or Sandy, which we like best."

In the uncomfortable silence that follows the boys snort and guffaw like any tweens when faced with uncertainty among the adults.

Milly quietly comments: "I prefer Milly."

"Then Milly it shall be," states Amos with finality.

When Esther starts to protest Samuel concurs with his eldest saying: "Milly it is, no arguing. Esther, boys, are we clear?"

Casting sidelong looks at Esther the boys nod while mumbling a reply. She ignores them but rolls her eyes and slumps back in her chair with a pout.

Milly looks at the girl for a long moment before sweetly thanking Samuel and apologizing to everyone for the confusion her name has caused. She doesn't see the speculative look Daniel casts her way.

Nora states: "Shakespeare got it right when he wrote: *a rose by any other name would smell as sweet.*"

Amos speaks again saying: "Before we drop the subject, did Esther say your full name is Melisandre? That's unusual. I've only ever heard it as a character in that TV show *Game of Thrones.*"

Smiling at him Milly confirms her mother read the books while carrying her and that's how she came by her name. "At least that's what I was told, but it makes sense."

"You must be very young!"

"No, I'm twenty. The first book in the series came out in the mid-nineties, you know."

"I never read the books, just saw the TV show. It was... quite a surprise for TV in the house."

"I've heard that but we didn't have a TV at home. Anyway, if I say my name is Melly people guess it's short for Melanie or Melissa or Amelia. When I tell them it's actually Melisandre they become... almost offended. It's kind of strange, but I suppose nobody likes to be wrong."

Esther has been sighing loudly throughout Milly's explanation, while the twins goggle, utterly shocked at the thought of growing up without a TV.

Turning towards the teenager Milly continues: "I think Sandy is a very pretty name, thank you, but I've gotten used to Milly."

The young girl's pout turns into a scowl as she mutters: "Whatever."

All three men say *Esther!* In various intonations and the girl's face twists in a mutinous glare.

Milly again studies her for a moment before adding: "My birthday is April 1st, April Fool's Day."

Esther looks up fighting a smile but her eyes are bright with amusement. When the twins burst into loud laughter Milly joins them and soon the whole table is chuckling and the mood is light again.

Not Left Penniless

The Reverend Stephen Smithson has been visiting to have *the bride and groom talk* with Amos and Nora and stayed on to share their light supper.

After a satisfying meal with pleasant conversation he stands saying:

"Thank you for that, Samuel. I wish I could stay longer but I have another appointment," he says glancing shyly at Milly.

She asks if he *really can't stay for dessert?* completely oblivious to his yearning look. Samuel doesn't miss it and smirks to himself once he realizes Daniel has noticed too.

Checking his watch the Reverend grimaces saying he's already running late and declines with obvious regret.

After he hurries off the family eat the apple crumble Milly baked. Amos and Nora are meeting up with friends but the rest of them move out to the porch instead of going their separate ways.

The adults carry their coffee and Milly brings out two icy-cold pitchers of lemonade since it's a sultry night.

The boys each down a glass before settling cross-legged with their fingers flying over their *Steam Deck* gaming consoles.

Esther puts down her coffee, a grown-up drink she doesn't really care for, in favor of the fruit juice made with lemons from their own trees. Perched on the wide railing and resting her back against a crossbeam she takes a big gulp before squeaking: "Ugh! This is so sour!"

"No, sweetheart, this is how lemonade is supposed to taste. You're too used to having it drowned in sugar. A tart drink like this is far more refreshing in the hot weather," explains her father.

"Yeah, Esther," says one of the boys. "It's really good."

His brother nods in agreement and Esther purses her mouth in a grimace, sulking over the lack of support she expected to get. She keeps sipping her drink, though.

Milly sits down with a contented sigh in the middle rocking-chair, between father and son.

Samuel chuckles saying: "It sounds like you're glad to be taking a load off, Milly."

Daniel doesn't say anything but his very stillness alerts Milly that he's listening carefully. "I find this heat enervating, I have no energy it seems."

"Well put your feet up and enjoy a relaxing break."

Milly smiles but before she can reply Esther is swinging her arms batting the air wildly while shrieking about a wasp. Micah jumps to his feet, he's the twin who's afraid of their bees so wasps terrify him. Getting up Daniel places his body between the buzzing insect and the kids.

"Don't swat at it or he'll release alarm pheromones calling on the rest of his family to join the fight," he calmly states while remaining still.

"But I'm scared of them, Daniel," says the boy backing further away.

"Well they do sting so keeping your distance is a good idea but unless there's food nearby the wasps aren't interested and will fly away of their own accord." Just as he finishes speaking the wasp circles upwards and speeds away.

Looking at Daniel in awe Milly declares: "Wasps terrify me."

His gaze softens for a very brief moment and he comments: "It's good the lemonade wasn't sugary-sweet or he'd never have left." Before his impassive mask is back in place.

Samuel's lips quirk into a small smile observing the drama of the youngsters around him.

Changing to a happier subject to take their minds off of flying stingers he remarks: "Stephen is so happy about performing Amos and Nora's wedding service. He told me he was worried she might be Catholic and want the ceremony somewhere else."

"We're Catholic," says Micah.

"But not really" adds Joshua. "Only Dad is."

At Milly's confused look Samuel explains: "The Young family are Catholics but there was a rift generations ago. My great-grandmother was Protestant and interfaith marriages were a problem in their day. The couple had to promise that their children would be baptized in the Catholic Church.

My great-grandmother had no close family I guess, because no one on her side objected to the Church wedding. She never converted to Catholicism but did have her children christened in the Church, as promised. The Youngs remain Catholic in name, lapsed Catholics I guess you'd say.

Both me and my cousin Jerry married Protestant wives but boys I didn't know you were baptized in the Church. My three are all Calvary Church."

"But you didn't join Calvary Church, did you?"

"No, I'm not a churchgoer, although Stephen does his best to convince me," Samuel chuckles. "He has become my closest friend in the five years that he's had the Church living in Sweet Berry Cove.

Before that, well I never really had a *best friend* other than Ruth, my wife. I've always enjoyed male companionship through the co-op but that's something altogether different. Ruth was everything to me," he says simply.

Milly sighs at the romanticism of Samuel still loving Ruth so much even though she's passed on. She shares what Miz Tally told her.

"Yes, Miz Tally was just as inquisitive back then as she is now but there's no harm to her, she just wants everyone to have a happily ever after. She told you the truth, once I saw Ruth I was hooked. I grew up in SLO and I–"

"SLO?"

"Oh sorry, that's what we locals call San Luis Obispo. I was a city boy."

"Oh, I never knew that... I guess I just figured you grew up here on this farm."

"No, this was Ruth's family's farm. When we met I'd just started at CalPoly, I was taking Agricultural Engineering, and came here to help out with a barn-raising and her parents welcomed me with open arms."

"Dad, I always thought you met Mom at a dance, I never knew about the barn-raising."

"It was a dance, too. See, the barn-raising part wasn't a whole construction - not the way the old-time Amish events were - it was just an exercise in community-spirit building as the finishing touches were added and then celebrated with a dance."

Turning his attention back to Milly Samuel adds: "Ruth always wanted to stay on the farm which was perfect for me. After we married the place gradually became known as the Young Farm and once the boys came along we made the name change official."

"Well isn't that something!"

Samuel chuckles at her look of bright interest. "I know some of your background, Milly, but I don't understand why there was no inheritance for you as the adopted daughter."

"Oh that's because I was never adopted," she explains. "Sunshine kind of lived like she was in her own little world. If she wanted something to be then... well, as far as she was concerned it was.

I don't know if that makes sense but, hmm, how to explain... okay, Sunshine didn't believe that the government or *the establishment* as she called it, had any kind of authority over her in the way she chose to live her life. She raised me as a daughter therefore..."

"Yet there was no provision made for you in her will?"

"That will was written years and years before I was even born, so no I wasn't included!" she laughs.

Daniel has fallen silent again, hearing the conversation but not participating, maybe not even listening. Milly thinks to herself that *it's always hard to tell with Daniel unless he's actually looking at you and he seems to shy away from making eye contact with me.*

Samuel isn't ready to give up the *rightful claim* fight arguing: "But surely there is a case to be made–"

"I don't have the money or the inclination for a court battle, especially with only an iffy outcome. Besides, I don't feel that I lost out. Sunshine already gave me a wonderful life, she certainly doesn't owe me anything in death!"

Apparently Daniel has been listening because he now asks who does benefit from the will.

"A=Funny enough not the person Sunshine expected, which was her younger sister, because she was already dead. However the lawyer tracked down a niece and a nephew who will share the estate between them."

Milly relates the story as the lawyer, Matt Ellison, explained it to her. "He said:

I'm really sorry about you not inheriting the house because I know Sunshine would have wanted it for you. Unfortunately as she grew older she thought estate planning would be a jinx which still is a pretty common superstition.

The only reason she even has a will is because many, many years ago, when I was just starting my legal studies, we decided as a group to make our wills so that we wouldn't die intestate and let The Man *get it all. The couples left their worldly goods to each other but people like Sunshine, who came from family wealth, chose a favorite family member.*

The heirs, who I don't think Sunshine even knew existed! are anxious to sell quickly but I explained about right of occupancy so you've got 60 days to vacate. The For Sale sign will go up right away though, so prospective buyers will be coming through to view the property. Do you think you can be situated within two months time?

And that's when I told him:

Reverend Johnson, from our Calvary Church, has got something lined up for me but it's out of town. He'll be by shortly to tell me all about it. Would you be willing... I mean, I know you're busy and your time is valuable but if you don't mind and he said, and I thought this was so nice, he said: I'm delighted to stay to hear what the reverend has to say. It's my privilege to advise you, Milly. Wasn't that kind of him?"

Samuel agrees adding that this lawyer sounds like one of the good guys.

"Oh he is," Milly asserts. "Mr. Ellison waited until Reverend Johnson came to explain all about the job in your Farm Shop and setting up a web-store for the farm. He said that you, Samuel, placed an ad in the Calvary Church circular which he saw and so he got in touch with Reverend Stephen Smithson to discuss it.

Reverend Johnson told me my bus fare would be paid which was a surprise. I asked *why would they pay my way just for a job interview?* and then Reverend Johnson said *there is no interview, the job is yours on my testimonial so you'll be moving directly there.*

Then Mr. Ellison asked *what if she doesn't like it?* but Reverend Smithson assured us both that *the Young's are wonderful people,* and you are, *who will treat me like a member of the family,* which you do, *and Sweet Berry Cove is a beautiful place,* which it definitely is.

Mr. Ellison assured me that I could always get hold of him if I wasn't happy here and said *with that in mind I have to say the arrangement sounds like an ideal fit for your circumstances.*

I confided that I was a little anxious about leaving everything familiar to venture out somewhere unknown and they both understood. But Mr. Ellison told me *there's no future for you living here amongst all of us elderly neighbors, Milly. You'll end up turning into an unpaid nurse and general dogsbody. Going from the commune to a rural farming community isn't a huge step into the real world but it is a first step.*"

The children give up pretending they haven't been listening and ask questions like *what's a dogsbody? what's a commune?* and *who is* The Man?

While Samuel answers them Milly recalls the rest of Mr. Ellison's comment, the part she's carefully keeping to herself: *you'll meet new people, young people, and who knows? maybe Sweet Berry Cove is where you'll fall in love.* At the time Milly remembers she rolled her eyes groaning o*h Mr. Ellison!* but secretly she was hoping that's exactly what would happen.

Milly dreams of raising a family in a loving household, the kind that comes from a happy marriage. She's never dated but only because she never had the opportunity.

The tough kids who showed up at Sunshine's place from time to time always treated her like a kid sister to look out for so none of them ever tried to take advantage. Milly was never exposed to anything nasty.

Sunshine made it quite clear that back in the commune's heyday she didn't subscribe to the practice of *free love* adding *I didn't want none of that messy drama or friction, just good friendships.*

The old woman wasn't one for affectionate displays and thinking back Milly couldn't recall ever being told she was loved, but the words didn't matter, she and Sunshine definitely shared a strong familial bond.

Samuel is still perplexed by the turn of events. "But surely this niece and nephew will do right by you? If this lawyer told them you were living there then they must know all about you and will want to see you looked after, not left penniless."

"No, why would they? I'm nothing to them and honestly I'm fine with it. And I've now got a bank account! Well I always had it but it was only in my name for convenience. Mr. Ellison said I could keep it and I had to explain it wasn't mine it was for the bills.

Sunshine would have money deposited each month to pay the household bills. Most of them were autopay but sometimes I needed to write a check. I looked after that sort of thing for Sunshine. Also I used the money to buy the groceries and gas up the old Beetle.

So then he said *this account is in your name only so whatever is there right now is yours, unless there are automatic withdrawals to come out?* and I explained that *no, they all come out on the second of the month but there's a lot of money in that account.* And I remember him smiling when I said that, I guess it isn't a lot of money to him but it is to me!"

"How much is there, Milly?"

"Esther, we don't question people about their money."

"Why not?" ask the twins in unison.

"It's just one of those rules of polite society."

"Oh la-di-dah," giggles one boy which set off the other one and soon the adults are laughing at their antics.

Uniquely Sweet Berry Cove

Returning from her walk one evening Milly sees Samuel sitting in the old rocker on the porch and plops down in the seat beside him. Turning towards her with a smile he asks how she's settling in with the web-store and she replies with enthusiasm.

"It's really caught on. People are buying dried fruits ahead of Christmas baking. Oh, and the jars of jellies and sauces that I decorated with a red and green gingham ribbons? they've turned into popular gift items.

I was thinking we could easily expand to adding some handcrafted goods like holiday napkins, for example. I haven't mentioned it to Nora because she's got way too much on her mind with the wedding but I'm sure she'll think up some good ideas as well.

I'm guessing there's a ladies sewing circle or something like that in Sweet Berry and they might be glad of selling their wares on consignment."

"I think there is something... yes, there is, but I don't know the details. Do you know anything about a quilting bee or some such thing, Daniel?"

Milly turns, surprised because she didn't hear Daniel arrive. He pushes off from the door-frame and ambles over to the porch swing. The Young's swing isn't suspended from the ceiling, instead it's a free-standing two-seater on wheels for easy moving. Daniel turns it now to form a triangle with their chairs before answering:

"There is something, yes, but I don't know anything about it. I'm sure Stephen will know, the group might even meet in that big room they've got in the Church basement."

"That's what I remembered!" exclaims Samuel. "There was mention of it in the Church circular. Now that the busy season is ending the group is starting up again and yes, you're right, they meet up at the Church. I'll mention this idea to Stephen tomorrow and no doubt he'll have it all in the works in a day or so. People do love their Christmas preparations and decorating is a big part of it."

"Speaking of which I'm going to make batches of fruit cake for those people who don't have the time to make their own–"

Samuel interrupts her with a regretful shake of head saying: "Um, sorry Milly but I'm afraid we can't sell product made with alcohol."

"Oh that's not a problem, there was no drinking where I grew up. Sunshine told me alcoholism ran in her family and she never wanted to take a chance.

No, I make my fruit cake with apple juice and I know I can get plenty of that here. In fact I'm sure I can bake a very popular fruit cake that people will enjoy year-round, not just at Christmas, because of all the wonderful organic ingredients you have.

You can market it as a healthy light alternative to the traditional weighty cakes. I helped Sunshine create a delicious recipe using whole wheat flour and substituting most of the butter with low-fat yogurt. With the local honey, apple juice, and a colorful mixture of fruit we'll have a product that is uniquely Sweet Berry Cove."

Milly's passionate speech has both men smiling, caught up in her excitement. Their fruit farm and Sweet Berry Cove's Farmers Cooperative is their life's work and they are justifiably proud of the nutritious food they produce.

"Well that's a relief, and your cake sounds delicious," comments Samuel.

"It is, I'll make some tomorrow and you can taste it yourselves."

"Tomorrow's the wedding, Milly," Samuel reminds her.

Now Daniel speaks up saying: "Yeah and fruitcake takes forever, right? When will it be ready to eat?"

Milly laughs telling them that once the fruit has soaked eight hours the cake can be ready in about an hour and a half. I'll see what I've got in the pantry and get it started overnight tonight. And I guarantee it won't be like any fruit cake you've ever tasted before, it will be a million times better! Moist and juicy and fruity."

"I'm getting hungry already," laughs Samuel and Milly immediately gets up offering to fetch him a slice of upside-down cake.

"No, no," he says just as Daniel asks: "Is that what we had for dessert?"

"Yes, there's about one-third of it left because Amos and Esther went to Luisa's for a meal and Esther didn't have any, remember?"

"My teenage daughter and her eternal diet," complains Samuel, shaking his head.

Daniel is definitely interested in that leftover piece. "It was really good, but I thought it was gingerbread?"

"It is gingerbread but it's called upside-down cake because the fruit, today I used peaches, is on the bottom," Milly explains.

"You young people have better digestion for a late snack than an old man does so I will say good night and leave you to your cake," Samuel tells them stretching when he gets up from his rocking-chair.

He enters the farmhouse quietly to avoid disturbing the sleeping inhabitants. They've all got a big day tomorrow.

After wishing him a good-night the two sit quietly until the silence becomes uncomfortable.

Milly gets to her feet with purpose saying: "Come in to the kitchen and you can have the last serving of cake while I get the dried fruit soaking. It's months since I've made a fruitcake and I can't wait to see your faces when you try it. It's always been good but with the ingredients I get here? it will be fantastic."

Daniel's grin lights up his face and Milly catches herself staring before she quickly turns away blushing furiously. Daniel notices her color and smiles thinking to himself *she really is a pretty girl.* He turns down her offer to make him some fresh whipped cream for a topping, saying the cake is delicious just as it comes.

A couple of hours later a sleepy Milly is snuggling into her bed, soothed by the sound of Nora's steady breathing. Tomorrow will be a busy, fun, and memorable day.

Milly says a silent prayer that Nora's father will show up to escort her down the aisle, that the new caterers won't let them down, and that everything runs smoothly, and everyone enjoys themselves.

Princess Bride

All brides are beautiful, thinks Milly when she catches her first glimpse of Nora, *but she is an absolute Princess today. Regal is the only word to describe her gown, her hair, and her posture but any formal queenliness is conquered by the loving look she's sharing with her Dad. She's 100 percent magical fairy princess bride.*

The doors of the rural church are left open to accommodate the overflow of well-wishers. Those locals too late to snag a seat inside gather on the porch and down the steps to hear the ceremony. They are the first to see the bride and her father who arrive in a sleek limousine.

The sun momentarily peeps out from the cloud cover but farmers never complain about a rain shower so nobody cares that the day is overcast. There's even a superstition about *rain on a wedding day is a lucky thing.*

Nora can't contain her joy at being escorted on her father's arm. She's become so used to the haunted look he usually wears that she's forgotten what a handsome man Fernando Perez is. Right now he's relaxed and happy with nothing nervy or rushed about his movements. He's stylish wearing a tux and comfortable riding in a luxury vehicle.

His beautiful daughter has all of his loving attention and she's basking in it. Fernando puts aside all of his regrets to revel in a pride so profound he thinks his heart might burst.

The official photographer/videographer is snapping up plenty of shots while onlookers hold up their phones to capture their own candid photos. After pausing to follow instructions to *look over here* and *smile for the camera* father and daughter enter the Calvary Church to the familiar strains of Mendelssohn's *Wedding March.*

The air is cool inside the rustic building despite the crowd packed into the well-worn pews. Beribboned bunches of fresh flowers are tied to every other row of seating and their heady perfume scents the air.

The swelling of the organ music can't cover the complimentary exclamations over what a stunning bride Nora is. She confidently walks down the aisle following Esther Young in pink chiffon and Luisa Bautista wearing mauve. Those colors match the sweet pea flowers in Nora's bouquet.

Nora barely glances at Reverend Smithson's beaming smile because she only has eyes for Amos who looks at her with appreciative wonder on his face. Even the best man, Daniel Young, is smiling widely. He has a tight hold on the wedding band in his pocket.

It's a short service with the marrying couple content to recite the standard vows. Their matrimonial kiss gets a little heated until a couple of wolf whistles are heard amongst the congregation's applause. Amos grins hugely and Nora blushes prettily as Mr. and Mrs. Young head out of the church arm-in-arm. Luisa and Daniel come next, followed by Esther and Peter, then the two fathers happily in conversation.

Daniel catches Milly's eye as he walks back down the aisle. He'd already noticed her while standing at his brother's side before the altar. He was able to watch her unobserved as her head swiveled from side-to-side looking at all the folks in their dressed-up clothes.

He saw that she had her eyes made-up and looked very pretty with the skillful shadowing making them appear even bluer and bigger than usual.

Milly is evidently excited to be in the church and she keeps whispering to Hannah Cairns who sits beside her. Now, despite the tears in her eyes, she has a huge smile on her face and he feels his lips twitch upwards in response. *What is it with females crying at weddings?* he wonders.

He catches her wiping away the traces of black mascara and decides he actually prefers her natural look.

Milly feels an unaccustomed fluttering in her chest when Daniel smiles at her. She tells herself it doesn't mean anything because he's smiling at everyone. It's part of his job as the best man, same as asking the ladies to dance at the reception will be... oh, that thought sets the butterflies fluttering.

Milly is delighted to be included in the evening's festivities, she didn't expect it but Nora insisted and Amos, mysteriously, said Peter would never forgive him if she didn't attend.

Under the photographer's direction the wedding party gathers In front of the church to pose in various groupings. They repeatedly have to call Esther back from visiting with the onlookers. The girl is making the most of her bridesmaid status and looks very pretty and quite grown up after having the hairstylist and make-up artist work their magic.

Even Luisa reveals there's a womanly figure under the flannels and denim she normally wears. She drew the line at having her hair curled but did agree to a make-up session that Nora assured her makes her eyes pop. Milly was invited to the grooming party as well, and is very pleased with the outcome – a very feminine look. She suspects she ruined her make-up when she cried happy tears during the ceremony but it was all just so magical.

The dinner guests journey from the church back to the Young's farm where the reception is being held on fragrant freshly mown lawns.

The meal is served right away in a huge open-sided tent that was erected while they were all at the church this morning. The tent comes with pastel draperies in case more coverage is needed. For now the gauze is tied back at intervals adding to the fairy tale ambience. Fortunately, other than a sprinkling of rain in the morning the dull day has remained dry with a mild temperature.

The decor matches the bridal party's pink-and-mauve color scheme, reflected in floral centerpieces, tablecloths and napkins, with an abundance of flowers banked on the head table and spilling over the edge. It's a lush, fresh, lightly scented display.

Milly sits at a table near the front with the fathers, Samuel and Fernando; the Reverend Stephen Smith; and Hannah accompanied by her husband Jim. They enjoy a generously portioned roast beef dinner with all the trimmings. Table service is swift and efficient.

Milly thinks of the sudden panic from two days ago when a substitute caterer had to be found after the original booking fell through. The emergency fill-in does an excellent job although Milly knows they charged an extremely high fee. Seeing how the guests are enjoying the meal Milly decides the cost is money well-spent, and certainly worth Nora's peace-of-mind.

Standing, but remaining at their table, Samuel gives the toast to the bride and the affection in his voice is genuine. Amos toasts the bridesmaids and Daniel, to Milly's surprise, delivers a humorous speech in a relaxed manner ending with *a toast to the happy couple.*

More photos are taken while the fancy cake is cut. That's done with decorum and no mugging for the camera or flicking icing in each other's faces. A dessert table is laid out and two coffee carafes, one regular and one decaf, are set out on each table as the dinner plates are cleared.

The DJ calls on Amos and Nora for the first dance. They perform a slow-speed two-step to an older country song, *5 Days in May* by

Blue Rodeo. It's still early evening and the sun hasn't set but the area designated for dancing is strung with white fairy lights for a magical effect.

At the urging of the DJ the rest of the wedding party joins in and everyone is entertained to see what a reluctant dancing pair Luisa and Daniel make. Then Fernando cuts in to claim a dance with his daughter amid cheers and applause.

Happy to get off the dance-floor Amos stands with Daniel and the two of them talk about how stunning Nora looks.

"She's like one of those Art Deco silhouettes: slender and tall," says Daniel.

"And lovely, and graceful, and my beautiful bride – at last!"

"You always knew she as the one, right from the start, didn't you?" Amos doesn't have to answer his brother with words, the sparkle in his eyes says it all.

Stephen invites Milly to dance and she's barely sat back down again when Amos is presenting Peter Showalty who asks for a dance as well. The music is upbeat and jazzy and they dance twice. Daniel intercepts Milly on her way back to the table. He's very obviously *doing his duty* and holds her stiffly with no conversation. Quite a contrast to Peter who had Milly giggling as he poked gentle fun at their fellow dancers.

After her four dances Milly is happy to sit with Hannah and Jim, who she met today for the first time, eating fresh fruit and a slice of tart apple pie.

"Jim aren't you going to take Hannah for a turn on the dance-floor?" Milly teases.

With a twinkle in his eye he tells her: "This isn't my type of music."

At Milly's inquiring look Hannah answers for her husband explaining: "Jim leads all the line-dancing when they're playing country pop. We've won dance contests but I have to admit it's all him, I just do my best to keep up!"

"Oh good for you! I've seen line-dancing performed but I've never done it."

"Oh we'll have you turnin' and two-steppin' in no time," says Jim with a wink.

Samuel has danced with Nora, Luisa, and Esther and he now calls Milly to the dance floor.

"I must say I thought the music would be a live band playing country tunes in a barn with lots of fiddling and square dancing," she says.

"Oh come winter you won't be disappointed. We have that very thing at harvest in October, then Thanksgiving, Christmas, New Year's, and any other excuse for a celebration in our down time."

"That sounds wonderful, Samuel. Jim and Hannah are going to teach me how to line-dance and I'm looking forward to it," Milly's eyes shine brightly at the thought of a busy social season and her pleased expression doesn't go unnoticed. Just then Esther interrupts their dance trying to cut in but she's unsteady on her feet.

"Esther, sweetheart, stand still. I've got you. Too much excitement, huh?" asks Samuel thinking his daughter has found being in the wedding party and sitting with the adults a bit too much.

"No it was the champagne I drank with the toasts," the girl replies with a hiccup that makes both Samuel and Milly chuckle knowing that simply isn't true.

"Sorry Milly, but I'm going to have cut our dance short and get this young lady home and tucked up in her bed."

"Well at least you don't have far to go!"

Esther flings her arms around his neck then sags as her legs give out. "Oh Daddy I can't walk!" she wails.

Milly hides her smile at Esther's attention-getting antics. None of the beverages served at the wedding have alcohol in them, not even the champagne or the sparkling cider.

Before her tears can start Samuel states: "Well then I guess I'll just have to give you a piggy-back ride, hmm?"

"Yes," she squeals, her age apparently dropping about ten years or so.

Milly can't help but notice how broad Samuel's back is as he stoops to let his daughter swarm on top. His sons get their size from their father and if they're lucky they'll age as well too. Milly gives them both a cheery wave as Samuel pretends to gallop to the farmhouse.

When she returns to their table more than half the guests are on their feet saying their *thank you and goodbyes*. It isn't late but early September is still a busy time in a farming community so the party breaks up soon after.

An old man with a shiny bald head tries to grab hold of Nora by the arm. He's worked himself up about something and can barely get the words out in his excitement. He stumbles, windmilling his arms to keep his precarious balance, he really is quite elderly. Milly sees both Amos and Daniel coming in quickly from different directions to intercept him. Fortunately his intentions are good although poorly timed.

"Miz Perez... whoopsy! I mean Mrs. Young... I'm sorry. I'm sorry I made things kinda difficult for you when you started at the school.

I'm man enough to own up and say I was wrong! I don't know why I thought, um... you know that granddaughter of mine? she's a little firecracker and the apple of my eye. I guess I was worried from all the talk or I thought... oh heck, I don't know what I thought but–"

"But everything is fine now, and your little Emmy sure does keep us on our toes she's that quick-witted, Mr. Sullivan."

Beaming, old man Sullivan mops at his bald head with an enormous handkerchief until Daniel takes hold of him, gently, and passes him on to Emmy's parents who hustle him away.

With that bit of excitement over and the last of the guests departing Nora tosses her bouquet. She's aimed it directly at Milly who can't help but claim the prize amid applause.

Miz Tally stops to admire the bouquet and ask the young woman if she enjoyed herself today.

"Oh yes, so much! This is my first wedding ever and everything was wonderful."

"Well my dear I'm looking forward to you and I having another nice chat. I warned you that I'm a nosy old lady and I've got some questions–" Janice Peart comes up to join them so Miz Tally says: "Ah, here's Janice to see me safely home. Milly, we'll continue this another time."

Amos and Nora walk hand-in-hand to the farmhouse to change into their traveling clothes. They've booked a ride-share to the San Luis Obispo County airport. It's almost a four-hour drive from Sweet Berry Cove to Los Angeles but only a little more than an hour's flying time.

Fortunately their ride is a roomy SUV for all the luggage they're taking on their lengthy cruise. Milly stays back from the family's farewells amid a flurry of hugs and kisses, but calls out her best wishes to the newlyweds for a wonderful trip.

After kissing the bride's cheek and shaking his brother's hand Daniel steps back and catches sight of Milly wearing the most forlorn look of longing he's ever seen. *Her heart really is with the newly married couple,* he thinks before noticing that isn't quite true. Milly's yearning gaze travels over Samuel who has returned without Esther, the twins with their parents and baby sister, and finally lands on himself. She jerks her head away before Daniel can read anything else in her expression but he's seen enough.

Milly's craving isn't for a wedding but for a family, a family of her own. That realization makes him resolve to be nicer to the young woman who must feel very lonely living as an outsider among strangers.

Milly turns back to wave at the retreating car. The first stage of the much-anticipated honeymoon cruise has begun.

The Young cousins depart amid the shouted goodbyes of the boys. The caterer's crew makes quick work of the clean-up and soon all that remains is the tent full of bare tables and stacked chairs. The rental company will be by first thing in the morning to pick everything up. Two minutes later everyone is gone.

Milly feels... she's not sure what, exactly. The wedding ceremony was beautiful and she really enjoyed herself at the reception. But now that everything's been dismantled and packed away, the music silenced and the guests departed, she's aware of an emptiness inside. A yearning for something... but she has no idea what.

She gives a rueful little laugh thinking that if she doesn't know what she wants then to feel that something is missing is just plain silly.

Turning towards the house Milly sees Daniel standing on the front porch smoking a cigar. She's never seen him smoke before but this is a special occasion. He watches her approach but as she draws near he hurriedly butts out his cigar before heading inside. Opening the screen-door he pauses for a moment then turns to call out a *good night, Milly* before disappearing from view.

Feeling reassured by his acknowledgment, even if it evidently was a second thought, Milly replies with a "Good night to you, too, Daniel," as she climbs the stairs and lets herself into the farmhouse.

She expects to lie awake for hours replaying the day's events and conversations in her mind but she's sound asleep as soon as her head touches the pillow.

A Seven-Day Wonder

The Young Family's Farm Shop isn't open today but Miz Tally is sure Milly will be working on online orders after closing for the day of the wedding. The lady has always been a frequent visitor to the Farm Shop since she fulfills the orders for its fresh-baked pies. The Young's give her a discount on the ingredients and she gives them a good price for the finished product.

Today isn't about business though, she's looking forward to having a heart-to-heart chat and learning all there is to know about Miss Milly Clarke.

Milly likes the old lady very much even if she does ask probing questions. Miz Tally herself warned Milly she would do so!

"Now my dear I'm an old woman who likes to know everything about everyone so come sit down for a minute and tell me where you're from, and who your people are, and how you ended up here in Sweet Berry Cove," says Miz Tally.

Milly smiles, unable to take offence at the honeyed Southern drawl of the elderly lady. Her eyes twinkle with enough goodwill and kindness to relax the much younger woman.

"I'm afraid I know very little about my people because I was raised in a foster home."

"Oh how sad! But surely there are records?"

"I'm afraid not, it wasn't an official place, it was privately run. Pretty much all I know is that my parents were killed when a drunk driver crashed into their car. I was only three and my maternal grandmother, Lizzie Sunderland, apparently my only remaining relative, took me in.

I have a photo of my parents, my grandmother had it nicely framed, from their wedding day. My father is wearing what I learned is called his *dress uniform* because he was an officer, a military man. Both of my parents were older people when they got married and it was implied that my birth was a surprise. That's pretty much everything I know and it's all second- no, third-hand gossip that was passed on to me years later."

Milly again tells the story she told Nora about how she came to be in the care of Sunshine nee Susan Forrester, although she only recently learned Sunshine's birth name, right up until the woman's death resulting in Milly needing to find a job and a place to live.

"Hmm, I wonder if this Susan was one of the Sacramento Forresters? Oh listen to me getting sidetracked so easily! Let's get back to you.

Now I know all about the *Help Wanted* ad Samuel put in the Church circular and how your Reverend Johnson got in touch with our Stephen. Of course the ladies of the Church were all agog! Oh my dear you wouldn't believe the excitement and speculation once we learned a new employee, and a young woman at that, was on her way to live and work in Sweet Berry Cove.

Everyone wanted to be the first to get a look at you! We just don't get many new people, especially youngsters, here."

"So am I still *a seven-day wonder* or am I *yesterday's news?* has my novelty already worn off?" inquires Milly with a laugh.

Miz Tally chuckles right back at her saying: "In Sweet Berry Cove? you'll be an object of interest for at least seven *years!*"

"Seven years from now I'll be twenty-seven," Milly muses, "I wonder if I'll still be living here then?"

Miz Tally reaches to take her hand saying with true affection: "Oh I do hope so, my dear Milly. I hope you'll live your life, a very long and happy life, here in Sweet Berry Cove."

For some inexplicable reason Milly tears up but she presses her lips tightly together to stop them trembling and instead squeezes the older woman's hand before moving around the counter to fuss over something unimportant.

She decides to turn the tables on her new friend asking: "That accent never originated in California so what's your story, Miz Tally?"

"Oh I'm an original Georgia peach," says the old lady with an exaggerated drawl. "And with a name like Tallulah where else would I ever go but to Hollywood?"

"You were an actress?"

"Well I tried to be one but mostly I was just a student going between acting and dancing classes with the rare audition thrown in. My parents had enough money to support me while pursuing my dream but I found out pretty soon that the competition was just too fierce. I mean that literally, too, honey because I encountered a lot of nastiness that was quite disillusioning to this starry-eyed girl."

Milly has a dreamy look on her face thinking about Miz Tally's adventures. "So how did you end up in Sweet Berry Cove?"

"Ah, that's a fun story! It happened because I walked into a particularly bad diner for lunch. It was a thing among all of us aspiring actresses to hang out at different lunch-counters, ever hopeful, because we'd all read in our fan magazines that Lana Turner got noticed by a famous talent scout – or was it a director? – sitting having a soda at Schwab's Drugstore–"

"Lana Turner?"

"Another famous platinum blonde," says Miz Tally archly, patting her curls. She smiles but inwardly mourns how her one-time idol has faded from public memory.

"This was my first time visiting this diner and after tasting the food I knew it would definitely be my last, as well. I was looking over the menu, they weren't pages long back then just one little laminated sheet, when a man sitting two stools down loudly whispered a warning to *stay away from the pie*.

I'd noticed how handsome he was when I sat down but I wasn't going to make things easy on him so I just ignored his comment.

When the server finally came over I ordered a sandwich and, defiantly, a slice of pie. As usual there was no variety, we customers always just accepted whatever was baked for that day, and it turned out it was apple. From the corner of my eye I could see that that man had finished his meal and was just sitting there smoking his cigarette and watching me.

I scooped up a big mouthful of apple pie and oh my goodness it was so awful I almost spit it right back out on my plate!"

Milly is laughing so hard at Miz Tally's dramatic re-telling of the tale she decides the woman would have been a great actress.

"He's sayin' *told ya so* and chuckling while I've got this horrible piece of soggy cardboard that feels like cement blocking my throat. I can't chew it and I can't swallow it so naturally I start choking on it. Next thing I know he's giving me a hard *whomp* between my shoulder blades and this horrid mass of chewy goo shoots back onto my plate. I'd have been horribly ashamed of myself if I wasn't so thankful to be drawing in a deep breath that I didn't care."

"Oh no, how embarrassing for you and you said he was handsome, too. Oh that was unfortunate!"

Chuckling now herself Miz Tally says: "Oh my Joel couldn't have cared less! He was all full of concern for me and my well-being and once he realized I truly was okay he started in lecturing me about how I should have listened to him as if he was my husband which is exactly what he became in no time at all."

"Really?!" exclaims Milly in delighted surprise.

"Uh-huh. I had met my future husband, a man visiting Hollywood from Sweet Berry Cove where his family farmed fruit. He knew his pies and that's why he'd warned me.

I had to explain that the reason I hadn't taken his warning seriously was because men try all kinds of silly come-ons and I didn't want to encourage a pick-up. He said he was sure such a beautiful girl had heard plenty of lines and, well... I was pretty much bowled over by him by then so that's how I ended up living here and living the happiest life with my Joel."

Milly's eyes are shining at the wonderful story. "Oh Miz Tally, that's just... oh!"

"And the same future might very well be here for you too, Milly, after all we have quite a few eligible bachelors for you to choose from."

Milly gasps in surprise but Miz Tally levels her with a look saying: "It's only natural, my dear."

Waving her hand as if shooing the conversation away Milly can't help but smile as she chides: "Honestly, Miz Tally. I've only been here a couple of weeks!"

"And in that time you've been noticed, and people are paying attention to who is doing the noticing. What do you think all that speculation was about?"

"Well since I didn't even know it was happening I didn't think anything about it at all!"

"You can laugh but well... if we weren't such a good Christian community I daresay people would be placing bets on–"

"MIZ TALLY!" interrupts a shocked Milly.

The bell over the door clangs just as an equally loud and nerve-jangling voice demands to know *what on earth is going on in here?* Janice Peart stands in the doorway, her inquisitive eyes flitting between the two women.

"I was just telling Milly there was plenty of speculation about who would be wooing her before she even arrived here, and now that we've all met her and seen what a pretty little thing she is the guessing has reached fever pitch."

Milly rolls her eyes but Janice Peart responds to her friend's comment dismissively: "Oh we all know Daniel Young will be the one she snags."

Milly's outraged *snags?!* is drowned out by Miz Tally's hoot: "Oh I do hope you're right Janice, but I don't think you're reckoning with just how stubborn Daniel is."

Janice Peart pooh-poohs that remark saying "Men are men, he won't stand by and let someone else snatch her up from under his very nose."

"I thought I was the one guilty of *snagging?*" asks Milly coolly but Janice doesn't take offense.

"Two healthy, good-looking young people thrown together? It follows as night from day."

"Well you couldn't be more wrong, Ms. Peart," replies Milly tartly. "I am not interested in *snagging Daniel Young* and I can heartily assure you that Daniel Young isn't the least bit interested in me. In fact, I'm quite sure he dislikes me very much!"

Miz Tally softly claps her hands and when Milly turns to glare at her sees the woman's eyes bright with excitement looking at something or someone behind Milly.

Feeling her stomach plummet she dreads looking but she has to see who is there. Slowly turning Milly is dismayed to find Daniel framed in the entrance. The bell didn't ring because Janice Peart left the door open.

He says nothing but at his quirked eyebrow Milly feels her cheeks flood with an embarrassing blush. She bites her lip as though holding words back before pivoting on her heel and hurrying through the *Employees Only* door to the hallway.

"Daniel!" exclaims Janice. "We were just talking about you and I said..." but the man doesn't stay to hear what it was Janice said or is now saying. Without a word to either lady he quickly strides through the same door following Milly.

She doesn't hear him approach and is mortified when he comes upon her standing with her palms pressed flat on the wall and her forehead resting against it. Hot tears stream out from under her closed eyelids. Daniel reacts without thinking taking hold of Milly's shoulder and turning her around to face him. The sight of her tears is unnerving enough that he regrets the impulse that sent him chasing after her because he can't pretend he hasn't seen she's crying.

"Milly, what's wrong? Why are you crying and why do you think I don't like you? Of course I do, I like you a lot. I mean as uh... as an employee, no as my co-worker. I don't *dislike* you..." he trails off uncertainly, afraid of saying the wrong thing and upsetting her even more.

Milly covers her face with her hands and hisses: "Go away, just please... just go away."

Daniel doesn't know what to do. Like so many men he's helpless against a woman's tears. Part of him thinks he should be comforting her while another part is more than willing to follow her instructions and just leave. He reaches his hand out tentatively to pat her but she flinches and jerks away so without another word he goes although with the dissatisfied feeling that he should be doing more.

Miz Tally tried her best to get Janice away, leaving the two young people *to sort it out themselves,* but she knew that was a forlorn hope. *I'm curious myself,* she acknowledges. So the women are just outside the staff door when Daniel comes through with a very confused look on his face. He ignores Janice's *what happened?* and lumbers out of the Farm Shop, pulling the door closed with a slam.

Facing those two women is the absolute last thing Milly wants to do but she can't give way to her emotions. She's been hired to do a job, not get all dramatic or be attention-seeking. Pulling a tissue from her pocket she scrubs at her face then blows her nose for good measure before marching back into the room.

She feels Janice's eyes, burning with nosy interest, on her but it's Miz Tally who speaks up saying: "We'll leave you now dear, and sorry about the upset."

Turning the old lady grabs Janice's elbow and drags her towards the door but before they make it there the woman actually digs her heels in, forcing them both to a standstill, and demands to have her say.

"Milly, don't you give up on Daniel Young. He thinks he's had his heart broken but it wasn't, just his pride got hurt because he knows, sure as shootin', that he had a lucky escape getting out from under that woman's clutches. Oh don't yank on my like that, Tally. Somebody's got to tell the girl what's what. I'd be saying the exact same thing to Daniel's face if he hadn't gone flyin' out of here in a rage."

"Oh, did he?" Milly asks, pretending a disinterest that both women see right through.

"Right well... now that Janice has spilled half the beans I guess I should complete the job. Otherwise things will be awkward between you and Daniel." Miz Tally inhales a deep breath and begins, reluctantly, to tell Milly the gossip that Nora wouldn't impart.

"Daniel has turned into a grouchy misogynist because of the way one flighty girl treated him and Janice is right: he's far better off without her and we're both certain he knows it, even if he uses the memory like a shield."

A small crease forms on Milly's brow. "He must have been awfully hurt if he's built up walls or, as you say, a shield."

"Hmmph, it's just pride. Men and their fragile egos," snipes Janice.

"No I think it was more than that, Janice," answers Miz Tally. "I'm sure Daniel truly thought he was in love and it's no surprise, Helena was – is – a beautiful girl."

Turning to Milly she explains that this Helena is *a tall, willowy blonde with cornflower-blue eyes and an enviable figure.* By time she finishes describing this paragon of beauty Milly feels depressingly dowdy.

"But Helen, I was at her christening and I refuse to call her by that fancified name she affects, anyways Helen's the perfect example of that old saw *beauty is only skin deep* because that girl has a nasty, conniving nature."

Shaking her head sadly Miz Tally agrees with Janice's assessment. "She was always quite clever at manipulating people, too—"

"Men, you mean," puts in Janice.

"Yes well women had nothing to offer her. Helena, and yes Janice I know what her parents named her but why not let her have something she thinks is better? Helena's father died when she was eleven or twelve, a particularly bad age for any kind of trauma especially with her being such a Daddy's girl, and her mother really had to struggle to make ends meet."

"Martha had a struggle from the moment she met and married Bryce Hannaford. He was a charmer, I'll give him that, but it was all show.

Champagne taste on a beer budget. I don't know how many people were left with empty pockets when he died. He was a smooth-talker and convinced a lot of folk who should have known better to back him in his harebrained get-rich-quick schemes. Afterwards some came crying to Martha but he left her nothing neither."

Her listeners took a moment to untangle that phrase, then Miz Tally continued saying: "It was all very hard on her and their daughter. I know Helena felt Bryce's loss very deeply and I'm sure it unsettled her emotionally. I think she found it hard to trust and hard to give her heart, or believe in good fortune when it came her way."

"That's as may be but the fact remains she latched on to Daniel Young when they were teenagers because he had plenty to offer. She dumped him when some slick carbon-copy of her Dad came along promising her fame and fortune. Foolish, foolish girl. But she'd never have made Daniel happy."

"No, I think you're right there. The fact, as you say, is that Bryce Hannaford's death tore a hole in his daughter's heart that no one will be able to fill because she won't let them. She really has had a sad life and we both know it won't last with that man she eloped with either. He certainly won't be able to make her happy."

Milly digests this story about people she doesn't know. She can't help but think what a contrast there is between the way she looks compared to the lovely Helena. She thinks this beauty must be foolish indeed not to celebrate the name Helen since it was Helen of Troy who possessed *the face that launched a thousand ships.*

After thinking a moment asks: "Do you think Daniel is waiting for Helena to come back to him?"

Miz Tally rejects that idea saying *definitely not!* just as Janice says she heard Helen is back in Sweet Berry Cove visiting her mother but she doesn't know if it's just a visit or something more. Miz Tally gives her a surprised look.

Don't All Girls Want To Get Married?

Once the evening meal is eaten, the fruit cake marveled over just as promised, and the kitchen tidied up again Milly goes out for a walk.

Starting from the kitchen yard she can either turn left to go through the orchards and growing fields, or right to cross over the wildflower field to get to the beach. Parts of the escarpment are too steep to climb down but as the land curves around the cove it drops gradually until rough pathways have been carved or, as she was told, a walker can continue to the far end where steps have been built for the villager's use.

Sometimes Milly takes this route into the village and joins many of her fellow citizens out for a stroll. Everyone exchanges greetings but almost none stop for a conversation. If they do it's only to ask a question about the wedding.

Milly understands that close-knit communities are slow to let newcomers in – it was the same at the commune where she grew up – but it makes her feel lonely. Nevertheless she's always careful to wear a cheerful smile, she came here to make friends and she's bound and determined to do so no matter how long it takes.

As the days pass Milly becomes a more familiar part of the village scene and soon children are greeting her by name while in turn she's greeting the dog-walker's pets by their names.

A few of the men have shown their interest in her. Reverend Stephen Smithson from the Calvary Church who comes by the farmhouse to visit Samuel often, and Jay Somers the man who runs the post office and general store with his twin sister Kay.

Milly is always uncomfortably conscious of Kay's eyes on her when she's in their store and comes away feeling she's somehow come up short in

Kay's estimation. And now Peter Showalty, the school principal, after several dances with her at the wedding ended up saying he'd like to take her out on a date. Those are the only men who have specifically shown an interest but she feels the gazes of others in the village, too.

This Sunday night she stays up top, having had a long day, and just enjoys the view of the ocean. It's been a busy time since she arrived in Sweet Berry Cove between learning how the Young Family's Farm Shop works and setting up the online store and, of course, helping where she could with the wedding preparations.

The time has flown by and she's enjoyed all of it. The Young's are a nice family, the Cove is a truly beautiful place to live, and her job is interesting.

Despite the bee-keeper's attractive clover fields plenty of bees travel to this field of wildflowers. Their gentle drone is a constant sound in Sweet Berry Cove. Milly steps carefully so she doesn't tread on the busy pollinators, knowing that honey bees are an essential part of the food chain.

A chill wind blows and she's glad of the cardigan she grabbed almost as an afterthought. The evening temperature is in the low seventies, but as a Californian born and bred Milly is sensitive to weather most people consider mild. It's always surprising to see the tourists wearing their shorts and sandals and halter-tops in much cooler temperatures than the local population would.

Milly's sweater is a fisherman's cable-knit in cotton that once belonged to Sunshine. It's lightweight and washable so it gets plenty of use.

Milly can still remember Sunshine trying to put the cardigan on and laughing her loud, belly-laugh when she discovered the buttons and their corresponding buttonholes were about a foot apart. She tossed it to Milly saying *there's still good wear in this so you might as well have it.*

Sunshine was always that way – doing you a favor but pretending it meant nothing.

The older woman had been eating healthy food for many years but she simply ate too much of it. Nuts and whole grains aren't lo-cal options, especially not when eaten with whole milk for the cereal and real butter on the bread. Sunshine always said she *couldn't abide margarine, even if it is plant-based.* But most of her weight gain was due to her excellent baking skills, an expertise she taught to Milly.

Daniel saw Milly on the path but he was off to the side and she didn't notice him. He wondered what was on her mind since her body language of head down and hands fisted into the patch pockets of her sweater showed she was bothered by something. When he saw her swipe a knuckle under her eye he started to move forward but caught himself in time.

Not my business if she's upset and crying, he told himself as he slowly backed up. But he stayed watching until she entered the farmhouse yard.

Daniel stood enjoying the cool breeze, just strong enough to keep pesky insects away, until his thoughts cleared and his mind was refreshingly empty. Turning, he headed back home and entered the kitchen where a low light burned all night.

At first he didn't realize anyone was there until he heard a rustling noise in the pantry. Coming through with a mug of tea Milly jumped, startled at the sight of him, but luckily didn't burn her hand when the hot liquid sloshed out onto the floor.

Daniel's *sorry!* mixes with Milly's gasp of fright. Her hand is still shaking so she comes right into the kitchen to place her drink on the table. Daniel swoops down to wipe up the small spill from the tile apologizing again. Milly watches him put the cloth back over the faucet and quietly replaces it with a clean cloth from the drawer before explaining it was all her fault. Daniel, notices what she does and appreciates her lack of fuss.

"I'd gone to get some milk for my tea and my thoughts were a million miles away. I didn't hear you come in."

"Yeah I try not to stomp around like a herd of elephants *all* the time..."

That makes her laugh and she looks at him gratefully. "My head was stuck back in the past enjoying my memories although I still feel so sad about losing Sunshine."

"Sunshine," he pauses over the name for a moment and though his face doesn't show his thoughts Milly can feel his disapproval, "was your guardian?"

"Yes, and she was a lovely person, a real caring and helpful do-gooder. Not a busybody or someone putting on a show, she loved helping people because she had a good heart."

Slightly taken aback by the fierceness in Milly's voice Daniel explains: "I didn't mean to imply anything–"

Milly immediately deflates, continuing in a much quieter voice: "No, I'm the one who overreacted – again! But people do judge her because of her name and I get it, it *is* a silly name for an elderly woman but it sure suited her nature. She was bright and cheerful and hopeful and helpful."

"Sounds like she was a good Christian woman."

"She was! except she wasn't a Christian. She practiced the Bahá'í faith which seemed to be more of a lifestyle than an actual practice. But actually," Milly gives a slight giggle and her tone becomes confiding as she says: "She joined all the churches in the area: Episcopalian,

Catholic, Baptist, and the Calvary Church she took me to, because of the social activities they offered for seniors, usually at a discounted rate too."

Daniel smiles back at her as he thinks of the old lady having to keep track of it all. He's glad to know Milly's tears were bittersweet and not heartbroken.

Last night he saw a different side to Milly in the party environment of the wedding reception. She was lively and excited, her color high and her eyes sparkling. When she danced her hair swung like a curtain and her limbs flowed loosely to the rhythm of the music. He'd become used to seeing the quiet, self-contained young woman competently doing her work but yesterday he saw Milly through the eyes of a man and couldn't help but notice how other men were looking at her as well.

There are very few unattached females in Sweet Berry Cove. It's common for couples to marry young, and those who don't usually leave for college or careers in the city.

Daniel never paid much attention to the girls in his age group because he was involved with Helena from grade school. Similarly he's never given any thought to the single men who live in the Cove now. Thinking for a moment he realizes there are several his age and older who might be in the market for a wife.

Watching Milly cautiously sipping her hot tea he wonders if she thinks about becoming somebody's wife. *Don't all girls want to get married?* he asks himself.

Maybe for Milly the Young Family's Farm Shop is merely a stepping stone in her journey into a wider world than the one she grew up in? He knows he's never going to get married but... he's disturbed to discover that the idea of Milly doing so bothers him.

His annoyed thoughts show on his face and Milly, looking up, sighs at the all-too-common sight of the frown he always seems to wear in her presence.

Something Wicked

The twins departed with their parents immediately after the wedding reception and the farmhouse seems very quiet now that the young boys are gone. No more calling to each other from different rooms, no feet thundering up and down the stairs, and no more electronic beeps from their video games.

It's Labor Day so Esther doesn't go back to school until tomorrow. She tags along when Milly goes to open the Farm Shop.

The shop is normally closed on a Monday since Sweet Berry Cove follows the tradition of no – or minimal – labor on Sundays. That means no baking for commercial purposes and therefore no fresh stock.

Milly has come over this morning to check what she's running low on, and to see what fruits have been left in the store room for her to use in today's food preparation.

The storefront's PoS software sends orders to the printer and Milly checks to see what's come in over the weekend. Determining how much work she has to do back in her kitchen Milly decides she can't spare the time to do any accounting today so doesn't bother logging in to the computer. Instead she gathers up the orders and her notes then looks for Esther so they can lock up and leave.

The bell over the door jangles signaling someone's arrival just as Esther cries out. Since her head is in the safe her shriek is muffled but still shrill enough to nab everyone's attention.

Milly hurries over to see what's upset the teen while the two women who had stepped into the shop just a minute before cry out: "What's happened?" and "What's wrong with the girl?"

Esther's eyes are like saucers and her mouth drops open with shock as she exclaims: "All the money is gone from the safe!"

A theft at the Young Family's Farm Shop! Milly turns ghostly pale as she pinches her lips together and breathes through her nose trying to quell her rising nausea.

"How much money was there?" demands Janice Peart poking her head forward to get a look at the safe's empty interior.

"Thousands and thousands!" wails Esther pressing her clasped hands to her chest in a classic pose of fear.

"Milly dear, sit down. You've had a shock and you look a little woozy," counsels Miz Tally. The elderly woman bustles forward reaching to take Milly's arm.

"I've had a shock!" insists Esther, but the sparkle in her eyes belies her words. She's excited by her starring role in the drama. *I couldn't have picked a better audience if I'd planned it,* she thinks triumphantly. *Nasty Janice Peart will see that this story spreads through the town like nobody's business. Milly won't be able to step outside without someone pointing a finger and calling her a thief. She's the only possible suspect. That Janice Peart will see to it that she's run out of town, back to where she came from.*

The jangle of the bell over the door draws the women's attention to Janice Peart coming inside with her cell-phone in hand smugly announcing that the police are on their way.

"What?!" cries Esther. "Why did you call them? We don't need the police!" Things were progressing faster and further than she'd planned. A bit of spiteful gossip was one thing but involving The Law well... that was entirely different. *Oh that Janice Peart is such a troublemaker!* she thinks angrily.

Sweet Berry Cove is too small a community to have it's own police force so when necessary the town calls on the State Troopers. An officer must have been in the area since the sound of a wailing siren soon shatters the bucolic peace on this September morning.

"Oh Janice," frets Miz Tally. "You shouldn't have called the emergency number."

"Nonsense!" Janice Peart retorts, "What's happened here is a felony and that means there's a dangerous criminal on the loose. A desperate man, maybe even a wanted man."

It seemed an unreasonably long wait between the slamming of the police car door and the arrival of the officer in the farm shop. Finally Miz Tally walks right up to open the door and wave a *yoo-hoo!*

Seeing the fluffy old dear framed in the doorway the man steps forward cautiously with his gun drawn but pointed at the ground. Puzzled he tells her: "We got a report of a robbery in progress?"

After casting an exasperated look at her friend Miz Tally enlightens the Trooper with an apology and a wealth of unsolicited and unnecessary information. Once he realizes there's no imminent danger he relaxes enough to holster his weapon.

Seeking to sort out who's who among the women he listens to even more explanations before learning one of the two older ladies provides baked goods to sell and the other is her friend and neighbor. The girl is Esther Young, daughter of the farmer who owns the shop, and the other is a brand-new employee called Milly Clarke.

Trooper Merkel gives the pretty young woman a reassuring smile after identifying her and asks what work she is doing, and how she came to get the job. Milly answers all of his questions easily but the tremble in her voice betrays that beneath her calm exterior she's feeling nervous.

Summing up he states: "So, you're not known personally to the family on the farm and you moved here specifically to get this job. You didn't know anyone in the community before you arrived, and you can't go back home."

While these facts are undeniably true they're distorted when strung together that way. Milly did come here not knowing anyone but it was on the recommendation of her local minister, and she can't go back home because her home no longer exists.

Milly is staring up at the policeman with a look of horror hearing how damning the facts sound against her. Just then Daniel comes through the door demanding to know *why are the police here?* and stops awkwardly upon seeing Milly's frightened face, unsure how to react.

When Esther blurts out: "We've been robbed and the police say it's an inside job." Daniel pulls back to scowl at his sister and question the sharp sound of Milly's indrawn breath before inspecting the empty safe for himself.

"Oh... oh no," he quietly states, seeing that Esther has told the truth.

"Can you give me an approximate idea of how much money has gone missing? We'll need to get an accurate accounting later, but a ballpark figure will do for now," says the Trooper, notepad in hand.

Rubbing his hands over his face a couple of times while thinking Daniel finally answers: "Fifteen to twenty thousand." The room goes deathly still, all the listeners taken by surprise.

Defensively Daniel explains: "We've all been really busy with the wedding going on so nobody's had a chance to take the deposit to the bank for probably 10 days, maybe even two weeks. Plus we keep a sizable float, way more than we need for a farm shop, but this is our only safe and we sometimes pay cash wages to day laborers so..." his voice trails off.

"Well, it's a crime, all right," says the Trooper. "When is the last time you can remember someone going into the safe?"

"I have no idea–"

"The caterers!" Esther excitedly interrupts. "Remember? the new ones wanted cash upfront!"

Daniel's face clears with the memory. "That's right! Two days before the wedding the caterer had to cancel the job. Some business disaster, I can't remember what exactly if I even knew, and there was a panic to find another caterer at such short notice."

"Oh yes, it was awful. Poor Nora was in a tizzy," puts in Milly. Turning towards the officer she explains: "Nora is Eleanora Perez – oh! she's Eleanora Young, now. It was a mad scramble to find someone who could do the job and because it was a rush they charged extra and wanted payment in advance to buy all the food."

"How much did they charge?" asks Janice Peart but she only receives frowns, glares, and a teenager's eye-roll in reply.

In the silence that follows her question Miz Tally speaks up saying: "They provided a wonderful spread. I would never have guessed it was a last-minute arrangement. What a blessing to have found them."

Daniel smiles at the elderly lady before continuing: "That means the amount of missing cash is less than I estimated. I wasn't here myself but I know the money to pay them came from the safe and it probably was taken out by my brother Amos, or maybe his wife Nora, on Thursday evening."

The trooper looks up from his note-taking. "What about the takings from Friday and the weekend?"

"We closed the Farm Shop those days. Everyone wanted to attend the wedding on Saturday and there was a lot to do on Friday."

"Yes, people kept dropping by with gifts and they all needed some refreshments–" begins Milly but Esther cuts in:

"And I had to make sure the clothes were ready to wear for everyone in the wedding party. I was chief bridesmaid, right after the Maid-of-Honor," she states proudly.

The Trooper is unsure how to reply to that remark so he just excuses himself to go make a call explaining, "I need to report this to divisional headquarters and get instructions."

This remark unfreezes the audience and the women turn to each other chattering and speculating. Daniel walks out, holding the door open for the officer who is right behind.

Startled by a loud cry of *oh, no!* from Miz Tally they whirl around to see Milly suddenly slump forward, falling off her chair and out cold.

Both men hurry forward but Daniel pulls himself up short watching while the Trooper kneels to check Milly's pulse and lift her eyelid.

"She's just fainted," announces the man, before asking: "Is there somewhere she can lie down?"

"Not out here," answers Daniel. "But there's a large armchair in the office, that's the room just through this door," he adds pointing the way.

"A chair's better than the floor so I'll carry her there." Daniel steps forward just as the Trooper scoops Milly up like a bridegroom. Daniel frowns but keeps walking to open the door and direct the man.

There are three doors in the short corridor: leading to a restroom; a room for storage; and the office. The women follow the men and watch over the proceedings of getting Milly settled in the chair, her head lolling back.

Janice Peart immediately comments: "I don't *think* she's faking it but... young women are artful, you can't never be sure about them." Studying the unconscious girl without a hint of sympathy she adds: "Well, Milly Clarke had the means and the opportunity so I'm sure you'll discover a motive during your investigations, Officer."

Miz Tally has come close enough to pick up Milly's hand and start rubbing it. She gasps at Janice's words asking: "Are you *accusing* this child of something? What exactly are you saying, Janice?"

"Oh c'mon Tally, it all hangs together and she's the only stranger here."

Envy, Malice...

State Trooper Merkel is crouched down at Milly's right side and Miz Tally has squashed onto the chair at her left but it's Daniel, standing down by her feet, who captures Milly's attention when her eyes flutter open. Their gaze connects but there are no answers in their wordless communication.

She was only out for a few minutes but his eyes are anxious until he sees she's okay. Then his face hardens and Milly is bewildered by a feeling of loss. She has no time to reason it out before the trooper is pelting her with questions.

"Why did you faint? What did I say that upset you? Is there something you want to tell me?"

Miz Tally protests that this isn't the time but Janice pipes up excitedly saying: "No, this is the best way to catch her off-guard, if she's not thinking straight she'll let something slip."

"Not thinking straight... that's exactly my point, Janice!" Miz Tally says indignantly.

Merkel asks Milly if she's ever been fingerprinted and she bursts out *no, and I've never even talked to anybody in authority, not for any reason, not ever.*

Miz Tally exclaims: "Of course the girl hasn't been fingerprinted, what a question!"

But just then Milly, wanting to be completely honest, says: "Well, I have talked to a lawyer but–"

"You have a lawyer? Why? Why did you need one? Do you think you need a lawyer now? Oh! I need to be very clear on this: are you asking for a lawyer right now?"

"NO!" she shouts. "I don't have a lawyer, Matt Ellison is a family friend. Except that I don't have any family but he was a close friend, a boyfriend I think, of Sunshine."

"Sunshine? Who's that?"

"She is... was... my guardian, I guess you'd call her. Then she died and Mr. Ellison, her lawyer, helped me get this job. He got a copy of my birth certificate and my Social Security Number and when Reverend Johnson told me about this job Mr. Ellison looked into it for me. He's always been very kind to me."

The girl is practically breathless from trying to get all the words out quickly to make the officer see.

"Mr. Ellison explained the house was being put on the market and I would have to leave because Sunshine hadn't made any provision for me in her will which was decades old but I never expected her to do anything anyhow, why would she? I was just an orphan she took in so she already gave me plenty."

She stops abruptly, deciding not to mention her bank account since she'd grown up with Sunshine's ddistrust of *The Man*, as the ex-flower child used to say.

By time she's finished her explanation Milly is panting, white-faced, and shaking. Esther starts to cry and yells for them to stop all their bullying.

Miz Tally looks worried, Janice Peart looks knowing, and the Trooper is puzzled. Daniel is conflicted, he wants to believe Milly but knows how untrustworthy women can be, and how easily they lie.

His neutrality is painful to Milly who resolves to harden her heart against caring how Daniel or any other man feels or thinks about her. It hurts to think this way but Milly realizes she can't rely on anyone else, she's entirely on her own.

Straightening up the officer says: "I apologize if you think I've been overly harsh ma'am, but these questions need to be asked and the sooner the better. I'll be passing everything on to my superiors and they'll determine what further action will be taken and... that's a lot of money that's gone missing so there will be something, for sure."

He nods to the older ladies then leaves the office and they hear the welcome bell ringing when he goes out the front door.

Daniel eyes Milly uncertainly, she really doesn't look well, but he hesitates to say anything. He doesn't want to give that Janice Peart even more to gossip about.

When Milly looks up he gruffly half-asks, half-states: "You'll be okay?" and she just nods, too weary with shock and sadness to speak. Daniel leaves her in the care of the women.

"Both of you girls have had a nasty shock so we're going to walk you back to the farmhouse, unless you have to get going, Janice?"

Miz Tally knows Janice is eager to go spread this morning's news. *Real news, not gossip,* thinks Janice excitedly, *because that theft really happened and I was there at the discovery. But what if the girl in her weakened state, and she does look awful, says something incriminating? I can't count on Tally to pick up on it... or to share if she does. These* thoughts race through Janice's mind so there's only a brief pause before she graciously offers to help get the girls home.

Milly's got a head full of speeding thoughts as well. Her mind can't seem to grab hold of an idea long enough to reason out if it's useful or worthless. She greatly disappoints Janice Peart by being so engaged internally that she doesn't utter another word. With her arms wrapped around her body and her shoulders hunched she doesn't look at all well.

Patting the young woman on the shoulder Miz Tally tells her: "Make yourself a nice cup of hot tea and then have a lie-down. Actually, take a nap first and then drink the tea to refresh you when you wake up."

"I need to lie down, too," whines Esther. Nodding at the girl the old woman agrees *that's an excellent idea.*

Milly and Esther go into the farmhouse and enter their respective bedrooms. Milly walks through the room to the bathroom where she shudders at her pale reflection.

She splashes water on her face to wash away all trace of tears but there's nothing she can do about her hollowed-out appearance. She has no intention of resting knowing her thoughts won't let her relax and she's far better off keeping busy. Besides, she's got all those online orders to fulfill.

Thankful that she had enough of her wits about her to bring home the bag of supplies, lemons, for today's baking she heads to her place of refuge.

Unfortunately Hannah will be in the kitchen, and will have to be told what has happened. With a sigh Milly realizes just how much she does *not* want to have that conversation but she has to, it would look very odd if she said nothing.

After brushing her hair Milly pinches her cheeks to add a bit of color before facing up to Hannah's inevitable questions. She walks downstairs briskly, ready to get to work.

Milly is inordinately relieved to find out that Daniel has already passed on the news. He'd actually come into the farmhouse searching for his father but after taking one look at his face Hannah demanded he tell her what was wrong. She is shocked and upset by the loss of that much money and wants to go over all the details again with Milly when she arrives.

Fortunately Milly is able to keep working with little need to contribute to the conversation while the housekeeper wonders and surmises.

Milly finds that performing the familiar tasks of making pastry, whipping up a meringue topping, freezing the leftover egg yolks for a peach crumble, and baking her lemon pies is soothing. For the family's dessert she prepares lemon pudding in individual bowls since there's just the four of them.

Samuel returns home well before dinner time and Daniel takes him into the sitting-room to discuss the situation. After the whole episode has been related and with many questions asked and answered – even if the answer is I *don't know* – Daniel tries to pinpoint exactly how he feels about everything. He's knotted up inside knowing this will bring trouble to the farm. The next while is going to be a difficult time for all of them. He cannot believe Milly Clarke is a thief but he has no other solution to offer.

Samuel is very angry about the implication against Milly. He phones up Reverend Smithson to discuss this with his close friend only to discover the news has already spread. Ending the call he turns around with a huge frown on his face.

"That Janice Peart has been all through the village telling everyone about the theft and the way that State Trooper questioned Milly. I'm going to call Ollie Mason and get his opinion."

"So you think Milly needs our lawyer?"

Samuel has a helpless look on his face when he says: "I really don't know. I guess it all hinges on what this officer's superior's decide to do. What did you think of him?"

"Well... he was stunned to learn how much money was in the safe, and it was much more than usual, but I explained about everyone being so busy with the wedding that no one went to the bank. He also seemed to believe everything that Janice Peart said as gospel–"

With a groan Samuel interrupts his son saying: "Why, of all the people in this community, did she have to be the one who was there?"

"Miz Tally was there too–"

But again Samuel interrupts: "Oh Tallulah's no problem, she thinks the best of everybody and won't tell tales."

"No, I meant it was good Miz Tally was there to kind of balance out what that Peart woman was saying. The trooper found it odd that Milly doesn't have any family and came here to live among strangers in an unfamiliar place."

Daniel pauses to think for a moment before adding: "I guess it is a bit strange."

"Not at all. I put an ad in the church circular and it got distributed to all the Calvary Churches in the region. The foster home where Milly was raised had closed several years before with Milly staying on as a companion helper to the elderly lady who owned the house. The Reverend there, um... Johnson, yes that's his name, Reverend Johnson, was going to recommend that Milly apply for the job and then this woman, Sunshine she called herself, suddenly died.

The Reverend looked on it all as a *the Lord giveth and the Lord taketh away* kind of thing and that's why Milly came straight to us sight unseen. From both her and our perspectives."

Daniel listens quietly and when his father finishes asks flat out: "So you don't think—"

"Not for a New York minute!" declares Samuel heatedly. "And you don't either. That girl's not only innocent she's also open and honest and good and sweet."

When Daniel lifts an eyebrow and gives a half-smile Samuel shakes his head saying: "Oh no, don't look at me like that son, I don't have designs on Milly. In fact, if I was inclined to be a matchmaker – which, thank goodness I'm not – I'd be looking at you."

"Me? Huh! no thank you."

"Oh! I thought you two got along okay?"

"Oh we do, I mean she's nice enough, but I'm not interested in her or anyone else. I learned my lesson and I'm not fool enough to repeat my mistakes."

"Oh Daniel, I thought you had more courage than that."

Shaking his head Daniel refuses to be baited by his father. "No you don't Dad, I'm not being drawn into an argument with you. If you're certain Milly wouldn't have stolen from us then what do we do to help her? or maybe we should just leave the investigating to the professionals?"

"I would if I was convinced they'd be fair but when we're dealing with the state troopers who don't know any of us very well sometimes expedient, rather than just, solutions are found. I'll give Ollie a call and make sure he's prepared to step in if Milly is arrested."

Esther, who has been eavesdropping, rushes into the room in a state exclaiming: "They can't arrest Milly, they just can't!"

Samuel hugs his daughter saying he's glad to hear her come to Milly's defense since he'd been under the impression that Esther didn't really like her.

"Oh well, we're not friends... I mean, she's older than me, but I don't believe she would do something like that... there must be another explanation!"

It's a shame that Milly wasn't eavesdropping as well because it would have done her peace of mind a world of good to hear Samuel say to his children: "I agree, my dear. I don't think Milly Clarke would steal from anyone, least of all us!"

...And All Uncharitableness

The farmhouse is very quiet during the day. After the whirlwind that is a teenage girl getting ready for school and always *almost* missing the bus the old home settles down.

Hannah, far more interested in cleaning than cooking, efficiently completes her tasks throughout the house. Daniel and Samuel are in and out of the place but mostly out. Milly works at the Farm Shop, making some sales and fulfilling the online orders, until mid-afternoon when she returns home to bake whatever she needs to replenish.

With school back in the biggest wave of tourists is over so the shop hours are 10:00 to 3:00. In the summer they'll work longer hours but both Esther and Nora will be there as well once the school-year ends.

Milly closes up for the lunch-hour when she goes back to the farmhouse for the hot meal Hannah has cooked. A daily meat dish of baked ham, roast turkey, roast beef, fried pork chops, or fried chicken – standard hearty fare for men who labor in the fields but Milly finds it too big of a meal for herself.

She stocked up on salad greens at the grocery store resolving to start up a kitchen garden like they had at Sunshine's place. Milly serves herself a slice of meat then fills her plate with what Hannah calls *that rabbit food* casting a disdainful eye over it. Milly has caught both Samuel and Daniel's interested looks and makes a point of placing a big bowl of salad on the table for the light meal they eat in the evening once Hannah has finished for the day and left.

When Milly asked why they never eat seafood *since we're right on the ocean* Hannah gives her a horrified look before crying: "Fish? Those nasty slimy things that swim in their own muck? Not in my kitchen! Not never!"

Milly doesn't want to upset the older woman or her routines, Hannah's been housekeeper at the farmhouse for many years, so she doesn't argue. *I'll just have to settle on ordering fish and chips on the rare occasions I actually go out for a meal,* she tells herself.

One afternoon Samuel and Milly are left lingering over their coffees when he startles her by asking what, specifically, is wrong. Both Hannah and Daniel have left so it's just the two of them and, to her great dismay, Milly bursts into tears.

Samuel slides his chair closer so he can slip an arm over her shoulders murmuring: "Oh my poor girl, I'm sorry, so sorry you're upset."

Milly allows herself to relax into the comfort of his embrace but only for a couple of minutes. Straightening up she hurriedly dashes her tears away, hiccups, and apologizes *for giving way.*

"Not at all, I want you to let it all out. I've been watching you struggle with the old *stiff upper lip* but my dear child you don't need to pretend with us."

"Oh I feel such a fool!" she exclaims, her voice still thick with the tears in her throat.

"No! not at all. Milly we're on your side, you're part of our family now."

The kindness of his words, said in such a gentle tone, devastate the girl. She lets loose a storm of weeping and buries her face against Samuel's chest. It's into this scene that Daniel returns, abruptly halting at the sight of his father holding Milly close.

His face turns first white with shock then red with embarrassment at what he's witnessing. Stumbling though a mumbled apology he edges away until his father's shout of "Daniel! Come back here, we need your help!" stops him.

Samuel beckons Daniel over and passes the sobbing girl into his son's arms explaining, "I'm not certain but I think the pressure and stress of all the gossip and suspicion has just built up to boiling point. I simply asked the poor child what was wrong... but it's good to get it all out," he adds, surveying the picture the two young people make with satisfaction.

Seeing this look Daniel frowns and loosens his hold. Almost as if she's waking up Milly pulls back with a dazed expression as she lifts her wet face to look into Daniel's eyes.

"Oh... OH! Oh no!" She ducks her head to hide her tear-stained cheeks and pushes him away. "I'm so sorry, please Daniel I... I'm just... I'm sorry."

Standing she turns to Samuel and gives him a tremulous smile as she explains: "Your kind words just did me in. It won't happen again, I... I feel better now that I've got all that emotional nonsense out."

Giving a fleeting, shameful glance at Daniel she adds: "So sorry," barely above a whisper before quickly leaving the room. The two men exchange concerned but helpless looks and sit silently with their own very different thoughts.

Schools in the farming community allow students some leeway in attendance during busy periods like harvest times. Since there's still plenty to do during the first weeks of September Esther's school lets out at noon.

At lunch she's full of stories from her first days back, about her teachers and who is in her classrooms, and what extracurricular activities she wants to sign up for, and it isn't until Hannah asks Milly if *she isn't hungry?* that the men notice she's hardly eaten a thing. This is a couple of days after Milly's tearful reaction and both father and son have carefully avoided saying anything to cause a repeat.

"Oh, sorry Hannah but no, I'm not especially hungry just now... although it sure looks good," she adds. Hannah just shrugs her shoulders and carrying her emptied plate away heads back to her chores.

Samuel expresses concern but Daniel studies her without saying a word. Milly fidgets under his gaze, finally forcing herself to scoop up and eat a forkful of mashed potatoes. She's very conscious of being under everyone's scrutiny but knows she can at least fix Esther's annoyance at losing the spotlight by asking:

"Is your best friend in the same classes as you? Oh! I guess it doesn't matter, I'm sure you've got plenty of friends."

Flattered Esther agrees that she is quite popular.

"Well Miss Popularity," Samuel says causing his daughter to giggle, "I want you to help Milly in the Farm Shop this afternoon."

"Dad, no!" complains the girl, just as Milly says: "Oh no, that's not a good... uh, um use of her time, it wasn't busy this morning."

"Then it might be busy this afternoon and if not the two of you can keep each other company."

"Oh yes that would be nice but I'm sure Esther has other things to do like... um... like homework!" insists Milly.

With a patriarchal air of finality Samuel states: "You're very pale and you've barely eaten, Milly, you might be coming down with something. I don't want you alone in the shop all afternoon. If Esther has homework she can take it along with her."

Milly seems ready to argue but Esther can tell when her father's mind is made up. She loudly sighs saying she'll *grab her tablet and then the two of them can walk over together.* When the girl leaves the room Milly tries one more time to say she's fine on her own but Samuel is adamant.

Daniel speaks up then asking if there's some reason Milly doesn't want Esther in the Farm Shop today? and she quickly replies *no, no, nothing like that.* Hearing Esther returning Milly hurries into the hall to avoid any further questions.

Once the two women have left father and son again exchange questioning looks but just shrug their shoulders at the mystery of females.

It isn't long before Esther is clued in to what's going on. She can't believe what she's seeing and hearing and it makes her feel sick. She's known these villagers, by sight at least, for her whole life but now her neighbors are acting like strangers.

The nasty whispering and muttered comments make the girl feel dirty, soiled by their despicable cruelty, yet nothing is said loud enough to respond to. *It's all so underhanded and.. and just plain terrible,* she thinks angrily.

Like that woman Margaret, Reverend Johnson's housekeeper, buying just one cheap item and making such a production of counting out her change. She wouldn't take it from Milly's hand so Milly laid it on the counter in a neat pile. Margaret scattered the coins and is now moving them around with one finger while she counts over and over again. Milly doesn't say a word, just stands there with her color high and her lips bloodless from being pressed together so tightly.

Apparently still not satisfied but unable to pinpoint why Margaret gives the coins a suspicious glare before sweeping them into her change purse and tut-tutting her way out the door.

The whole line of customers, yes most unusually there actually is a line in the Young Family's Farm Shop, has watched Margaret's performance with avid interest. She's planted a seed in their minds and every person makes a point of checking and double-checking their change. Except that widow lady, Esther can't remember her name, who takes her turn at the till empty-handed.

"I'm here to close my account. I want a printed statement, which I will check carefully before paying, and then this establishment won't get another penny from me," she declares, pursing her lips and giving her head a sharp nod.

"The loss of your pennies isn't going to bankrupt the Youngs, Edie," calls out a loud male voice from the doorway. The man strides into the shop and Esther exchanges a fearful look with Milly, recognizing him as the odd, old fellow who accosted Nora at the wedding.

"I fell for the vile rumors you women spread once before and more fool me, but I've got your number now. It's wickedness, just as it says in Proverbs: *A perverse person stirs up conflict, and a gossip separates close friends.* So if you only came in here today to gawk and make a couple of defenseless girls miserable you can leave right now."

Old man Sullivan is causing a scene with his tone of voice belligerent and his elderly body quivering with righteous anger as he holds the door open wide.

"You're not one of the Youngs! so what gives you the right to tell us what we can and cannot do?" cries a carefully made-up woman, her raucous voice contrasting with her expensive outfit.

Jackson Sullivan, now very red in the face, bawls at her: "I'm a friend of the family, that's who I am. And you..." looking her up and down he practically spits: "You're some jumped-up nobody dressed to the nines in her dead husband's insurance money."

A ripple of electrified shock runs through everyone in the shop until a familiar voice calls out: "Jackie that's not a nice thing to repeat even if it is true. Now you've said your piece – and very well too, I must add – but come on out of here now. Let the shoppers finish their business and let the gawkers slink away."

Miz Tally has come up to stand beside him in the doorway casting her eye over the assemblage. No one is willing to tangle with her and after old Mr. Sullivan doffs his cap in acknowledgment he exits, closely followed by several others.

The remaining shoppers complete their purchases without comment and soon only the three women remain, each shaken – although in different ways – by what happened. Finally Milly breaks the silence by thanking Miz Tally for her assistance.

"I heard a couple of remarks in the village that made me think some folks might be up to no good so I felt I should come by."

"Well I'm very glad you did. I'd like to invite you back to the farmhouse for a cup of tea and cake but... can I ask you not to say anything about this to Samuel?"

"Oh I'll never say no to your cake, Milly but I will say no to keeping quiet about this. Samuel needs to know what went on here this afternoon and frankly I don't think you girls should be here on your own."

"Milly!" exclaims Esther, "Was it like that this morning too? Is that why you told Dad I shouldn't come?"

The young woman rubs her fingertips across her brow as if she's trying to massage a headache away. "It's been this way ever since... well, it's ugly but no one comes right out and asks a question or makes an accusation I can answer! It's all just... just something I can't defend against."

She looks ready to cry tears of frustration and Esther feels badly for what Milly is going through. She would never have believed adults could act like this. She's witnessed some bullying at school but that always happens between kids with a teacher quick to intervene. This is something different... and disturbing.

"Why don't you lock up now and we'll all head back together. A restoring cup of tea is exactly what we need for now, and for later... well I'm confident it will all work out."

"Oh it will, I'm sure it will," agrees Esther adding: "Everyone has just blown this thing right out of proportion. It's all because that Janice Peart called the police! Nobody asked her to."

"Well it really is a lot of money, Esther," says Milly giving the girl an odd look before realizing Esther has never had to pay bills or watch her spending so the loss doesn't have the same impact. She links arms with Esther and Miz Tally and although she's dreading the forthcoming confrontation she accepts that it's unavoidable.

Samuel and Daniel both go straight to change their clothes and wash up when they come in from the fields, finished for the day. Four women in varying degrees of upset are waiting for them when they get to the kitchen. The remains of a snack lies on the table and Hannah clears it away while Milly sets the kettle to boil for a fresh pot of tea.

They leave it to Miz Tally to tell the tale, knowing the men are more likely to behave themselves in deference to the elderly woman. Still, Samuel pounds the table in anger while Daniel goes very still with his eyes mere slits as he grinds out the question of *who was there?*

Sidestepping his inquiry Miz Tally relates how Jackson Sullivan had things well in hand by time she arrived. Between them they cleared the shop and she escorted the girls home.

Speaking for the first time since they got home Milly carefully explains: "Nobody came and say anything outright, just whispers and innuendo, no threats of violence or anything like that."

"But it was like that this morning too, wasn't it Milly?" says Esther turning to support the other woman. Seeing how Milly's eyes widen Esther realizes she's made a tactical error just as Daniel's voice sounding deeper and colder than usual cuts in harshly asking: "Why didn't you say anything about this to us at lunch-time?"

Stung by the unfairness of his anger Milly snaps back: "I was dealing with it. Besides, it's my problem, not yours."

"But you exposed my sister to it!" he shouts.

Milly hates that she's crying but she can't stop the tears from flowing. "I'm really sorry about that Esther, Samuel. I tried to say something but then I thought maybe... maybe if Esther was there they'd just go away. I'm so sorry," and pushing back she evades Miz Tally's outstretched hand and pounds up the stairs to her room.

Hannah seethes: "Daniel Young what is the matter with you?"

Samuel angrily adds: "You owe that girl an apology."

Daniel looks into the faces of all four of the people in the room and finds no understanding or sympathy. With an explosive "Huh!" he goes barreling out the kitchen door. Moments later they hear the unmistakable sound of his ancient pick-up truck racing out of the yard.

"These young people..." Miz Tally lets the sentence trail off as she stands to leave. Hannah grabs her bag saying she'll be off as well and she'll see Miz Tally gets home okay.

"What a day you've had, Esther. Do you want to stay home from school tomorrow?"

"No, I think I'd rather go and find out what people are saying. My friends will tell me but not unless I ask. If I know what's being said I can put them straight!" she says, standing up.

Samuel gives her a quick hug saying *that's my girl*. Esther looks up at him and half-whispers "Oh Dad, those people today were awful, just awful to poor Milly."

He thinks a moment before answering: "There are many, many benefits to living in a small close-knit community like Sweet Berry Cove my dear but, unfortunately, there are a few drawbacks as well. I'm sorry you had to witness that today but... you're growing up, Esther. You can only control your own behavior, you're not responsible for the way anyone else acts."

The girl opens her mouth as if to say something more but stops and simply nods and goes to her room.

Samuel surprises everyone next morning at breakfast by showing them a *Closed Until Further Notice* sign he printed out on his office computer. He announces that he's going to post it on the Farm Shop door.

Serving up platters of fresh-made pancakes with sausages browned to perfection Milly tells Samuel: "Really, you don't need to shut up the business. I was a bit overwhelmed yesterday but now that everyone will know what has happened it should be okay. I certainly won't be blindsided and can deal with it."

"You shouldn't have to, my dear. It's the customers who will have to do without and maybe then they'll better appreciate having fresh produce and baked goods right on their doorstep."

"I'll still have to fulfill any online orders that come in," says.

"Please wait until this afternoon when Esther is home and can go over with you. I don't want you in the shop alone just now."

"I'll take you," states Daniel, much to everyone's surprise and Milly's delight after the way he yelled at her yesterday. It must mean he's gotten over his anger with her.

She looks at him with a bright, smiling face that he spends a moment admiring before adding in a deprecating manner: "You'll keep the door locked and people will see Dad's sign. I'll be working in the apple orchard so I can keep an eye on things, just in case anyone tries to come in."

Milly thanks him and though she spends the rest of breakfast with her eyes on her plate she eats with a good appetite. Samuel gives his son a smile and a nod of satisfaction before leaving with his sign.

Milly and Daniel's good feeling vanishes half an hour later when they arrive at the shop to find Samuel breaking up a board on which a vandal has spray-painted *theif go away.*

"Oh sorry Milly, I was hoping to dispose of this before you arrived. But I have to say I'm really not worried by it. The miscreant can't spell, and not spray-painting the walls or windows means he or she or they aren't out to damage property so they certainly won't hurt anyone, physically that is.

No, it looks to me like somebody acting out a dare among teenagers. I can't even begin to guess who but I suspect the offspring of someone who was thwarted from making trouble yesterday. That same someone might have complained at the dinner table and planted ideas of mischief."

"I'll bet Peter Showalty could give us a lead on who it's likely to be. Even if they've moved from the primary to the high-school he'll know who the local troublemakers are." Daniel's fingers are clenching as if he's imagining getting hold of the spray-painter and giving him a good shake – or more!

"You're probably right son but... do we even want to even acknowledge the graffiti? Maybe we'd be wiser to ignore it."

"Oh I agree, Samuel. It might only encourage others," says Milly. Her voice is steady but when she first spotted the sign both men heard her gasp of dismay and saw the color drain from her face.

Daniel gets a stubborn look on his face and decides to contact the State Trooper detachment to pass on the events of yesterday and today. Maybe officers asking questions will be enough to scare off the bullies and if not, well, he's pretty good at finding things out and taking appropriate action. He decides to keep his plans to himself, though.

When the family gathers again at lunchtime Milly confirms there were no problems at the shop at all. Daniel advises that only a handful of people turned up and after grumbling when they read the sign they turned away without any issues. Milly said the shop received a gratifying number of online orders so, with Esther's help, they can get them packed and ready for the courier to pick up.

Esther is agreeable, warning: "If *that Janice Peart* shows up and ignoring the sign starts knocking on the door I will take great delight in snubbing the gossipy woman!" which makes the rest of them chuckle at the picture she presents.

Here There Be Dragons

No one could miss the undercurrent of excitement running through the congregation and Milly wonders what is going on. There's no one she can ask. Esther has met up with a girlfriend to sit with, and the young cousins are back home, now so Milly is by herself. Looking around she sees angry glares and accusing stares but still doesn't understand... until suddenly she does.

Her immediate reaction is to shrink inwards, hunching her shoulders against the assault of muttered condemnation. Then Daniel appears nudging her none too gently to slide over and make room for him to sit down. He usually doesn't join them in the family pew, often not coming into the church until the service had already begun and standing at the back. But nothing is usual about today.

Leaning down he whispers in her ear: "Here there be dragons!" forcing her to stifle a surprised chuckle.

When the members stand for the hymns Daniel's rich bass voice rings out confidently. Startled Milly glances up at him but he keeps facing forward. Before she looks away his eyes swivel to meet hers and he quickly drops her a wink. She has to stop singing when her throat constricts with emotion.

Afterwards they sit silently until Miz Tally comes over and Daniel takes the opportunity to slip away.

The old lady causes a bit of a scene by grasping Milly's hand and loudly declaring: "I knew that rumor of you being arrested was pure hogwash of the Janice Peart variety. I never heard anything so foolish in my life. As if you would... tut-tut-tut."

She leans in for a kiss and pats Milly's shoulder before her niece helps her down the aisle. Milly is frozen with hurt at the censure of the congregation that prevents, thankfully, the hysterical laughter threatening to bubble up to the surface.

She's decided to sit waiting until the church empties out and everyone is gone so she can walk home by herself. Milly is appalled at the way people stared and glared so boldly. Some were whispering but most didn't bother lowering their voices as they sneered at her, the ingrate, the incomer, the stranger.

Being vilified at the Young Family's Farm Shop is one thing, but she expected better of churchgoers. She'd like to slip out without having to face the sympathy of Reverend Smithson but knows that's impossible. Thankfully he simply clasps her hand with a grave expression on his face and doesn't keep her standing there.

Walking out of the church on stiff legs she forces her shoulders back and pulls her chin up. Unhappily she notes that quite a few people are loitering, all looking her way. To her surprise Daniel comes up and she realizes he's been waiting for her.

Gripping her elbow quite tightly he puts himself between her and the villagers, steering the two them towards the farm. *If only the warmth he displays, holding me tucked into his side, was real instead of just for show*, she thinks dejectedly.

Milly is desperate to hold back her tears. Anger is radiating from Daniel and she doesn't want to upset him further. Both are fighting internal battles and neither of them speak.

After barely eating a bite of lunch Milly goes to her usual chair on the porch and rocks a bit. Then she moves to sit on the steps to catch the sun's rays, enjoying the warmth on her upturned face.

From this vantage point she can see Daniel approaching the farmhouse. She doesn't miss how he hesitates a moment before striding forward with renewed speed. He has to pass her on the stairs and she takes advantage of that, sticking out her arm to block him. He stops, turning his scowling face to look down at her.

In a soft voice Milly tells him: "Daniel, I just want to say I appreciated your kind support at Church this morning–" But he cuts her off sharply.

"Don't be," Daniel retorts, "because there's nothing to appreciate. I didn't do it for you but for the family. We all live in this village, Esther goes to school, Nora goes out to work, and Dad is busy with the co-op, so of course we present a united front. The Young name means something to us and to this community and we aren't going to let you wreck it."

The only sound Milly makes is the gasp of her quickly indrawn breath. The tone of Daniel's voice cuts right through her and his words hurt her deeply. He was so kind in the church but now... why does he run so hot and cold? Is it his problem or is it hers? What does she do to provoke this kind of reaction from him?

Milly wasn't aware of how much she cares about the Young family and their home here in Sweet Berry Cove. A place she realizes she'd like to be her permanent home too. At least she did, before all this unpleasant, bad feeling and cruel behavior.

She doesn't know what to say so she simply withdraws her arm and gives a tight nod before turning her head away.

Although only half her face can be seen from this viewpoint Daniel sees Milly's lips tremble before closing tightly and her chin tilt up with resolve. His thoughts are flip-flopping between regret for his harsh words, determination to keep Milly at arm's length, admiration of her self-respect, and a foolish wish to see her collapse in tears so he can give her comfort in his arms. Shaking his head at that last image he moves past her and goes into the farmhouse.

Milly follows at a safe distance and once she's safely away from prying eyes her tears gush forth. In the privacy of her bedroom she falls onto the bed and sobs into her pillow trying to muffle the sound.

Hearing footsteps pause outside the door she struggles to stifle her cries and silently begs the unknown person to *keep going, please just go, please go!* Thankfully there is no knock but perversely, Milly feels even sorrier for herself thinking no one wants to give comfort.

She cries till her eyes are streaming and her nose is plugged. Forced to get up for a tissue Milly's thoughts move from sadness to resentment at the unfair treatment she received in church today. *I didn't take that money and people shouldn't just jump to conclusions. The way I'm being treated well... it's just not right.*

Sulking morphs into indignation and Milly gives her head a sharp nod thinking: *where's my backbone? I know I didn't steal anything and I refuse to let their narrowmindedness get to me.*

After washing her face Milly carefully powders over the redness around her eyes and nose. Taking her long hair out of the ponytail she gives in a thorough brushing, pleased to see how the auburn highlights gleam. That small prideful pleasure is enough to boost her spirits.

The shadows are stretching across the room and she thinks it must be early evening by now. Although she hasn't had anything since breakfast Milly still doesn't feel like eating. She decides to get outside for a walk while it's still daylight. *Maybe I can work up an appetite?* she hopes.

When Milly steps through onto the porch a delightful scene greets her. Daniel and a stranger are smiling over the antics of a frolicking dog.

The creature yips excitedly as it races around their feet, it's too-big paws skidding as it circles them.

So entranced she forgets their words from earlier Milly rushes forward exclaiming *who is this cutie?* before dropping to her knees and getting a face full of wet doggie kisses.

"I'll leave you all to get acquainted now, Daniel," the man says as he moves back to his truck. Nodding, Daniel helps him unload the dog's cage from the back of the pick-up. The dog darts inside, grabs its blanket and rushes out again. The two men shake hands and then the breeder drives away.

The three of them watch the departing vehicle for a moment before the dog starts running and trips after tangling itself up in the blanket. Daniel scoops up the animal, dusty blanket as well, and owner and pet commune while grinning at each other.

"He's beautiful! What is he? Is he a he?" Milly is full of questions.

"Yes, he's a dog, a Saint Bernard puppy."

"This is a puppy? Really? But he's so big already!"

Daniel chuckles saying: "He's going to get a lot bigger than this."

"Well he's just precious!" Reaching to scratch under the dog's chin Milly asks him: "Who's a handsome boy, hmm?" The dog barks just as if he's answering.

"This is such a surprise, Daniel. Did you just buy him today?"

"No, there was an ad in the local paper saying a litter was due so I arranged to get this little fella even before he was born."

"Does he have a name?"

"No, they let the owners choose. I mean, he's got his show-dog name from the breeders because he's a pure-bred but I won't be using that. I didn't buy the breeding rights because this little guy is going to be a pet. He'll have to be neutered but we'll wait until he's a year old before doing that."

"So what are you going to call him?" Milly asks impatiently.

Looking at the puppy squirming in his arms Daniel thinks for just a moment before answering: "Bernie."

"Bernie? What kind of a name is that? He should be a Napoleon or Emperor or something majestic."

Daniel gives a half-smile as he shakes his head saying "Saint Bernard equals Bernie, makes sense."

"Poor Bernie," coos Milly, nose-to-nose with the puppy, "Daddy isn't doing right by you."

"Yeah well, don't get any ideas, eh? Don't steal him from me, okay?"

Milly pulls back so sharply Daniel realizes she's misunderstood what he meant and he regrets how his words have hurt her. "That's not what... I didn't mean that the way it sounded..."

In the tense moment he unwittingly tightens his grip and Bernie gives a little whimper. Both of them react, soothing the dog with soft words.

Milly feels an unaccustomed fury rise up inside her at his unfairness but she tamps it down. Looking Daniel in the eye she calmly states: "The truth will come out eventually," before giving Bernie one last light bop on his nose and heading back indoors.

Once she's away from the infuriating man she marvels at how he can rile her. *All those years living a placid life with Sunshine and never once feeling anger like this, but just a couple of weeks around Daniel and I'm ready to resort to violence!*

Behind her she can hear Esther's shrill cries of joy at meeting the family's new puppy.

Caught in the Act!

"Oh no! Drat me and my terrible memory, honestly I'm starting to think I've got *Old Timer's Disease!*" exclaims Hannah.

She looks up just as Milly comes into the kitchen carrying a big bowl covered with a tea-towel. It's heavy and Milly concentrates on placing it safely on the table before turning her attention to the housekeeper.

"What's Old Timer's Disease?" she asks.

"It's a bad joke is what it is. It's just a silly way of saying Alzheimer's Disease."

Hannah is only giving half her mind to their conversation obviously preoccupied with her concerns.

"Ah, the loss of brain function, yes. I guess poking fun is supposed to make it less scary? Sort of like *whistling past the graveyard?*"

The housekeeper gives a surprised look as she exclaims "Milly! you're too young to know an expression like that."

"You forget that I was raised in a community of seniors and retirees."

"See? I'm forgetting everything these days!" Hannah replies shaking her head in frustration.

"You never actually said what you did forget–"

Hannah flings up her arm dramatically pointing her finger at the full laundry basket sitting on a kitchen chair. "Daniel's clean clothes, that's all. And the thing is it's early-closing today and I must get to the pharmacy to pick up Jim's prescription but I'll be cutting it close even if I leave right now–"

Pushing the older woman out the door Milly insists she get going: "Go on, I can deal with Daniel's things," she says as she waves off Hannah's thanks.

Shaking her head over the older woman's histrionics Milly tells herself that the risen dough can certainly wait for the ten or fifteen minutes it will take to put the clothes away before they get all wrinkled.

Grabbing the basket by its handles she walks up the one flight to the bedroom floor. Daniel's room is at the end and opposite side of the hall from Milly's bedroom. She saw him go out this morning but nevertheless knocks at his door, even though it's slightly ajar, before nudging it open with the basket.

She hasn't been in here before, naturally she's had no reason, so she looks around with interest. It's tidy with a masculine color scheme of blue and gray fabric over mahogany furniture. There are some framed line drawings hanging on the far wall that she'd love to look at more closely but decides, with regret, that that would be too nosy.

After a moment of uncertain hesitation Milly starts opening the drawers of the low-boy dresser to find out where Daniel's socks, underwear, and t-shirts live. Feeling intrusive she quickly starts putting the items in their proper spots, re-folding a crushed tee.

Feeling more comfortable now that the man's *unmentionables* have been dealt with Milly opens both doors of the free-standing wardrobe. After hanging up the half-dozen shirts all that's left in the bottom of the basket are a couple of pairs of blue jeans. She can see a neat pile of denims stacked on the top shelf of the wardrobe, but unfortunately Milly is only 5-foot tall.

The base of the wardrobe is solid wood so she isn't worried about standing on it and breaking through but there's only a few inches of space in front of the built-in drawers. There's not even enough room to hold the balls of her feet so she'll have to grip with her toes.

Stepping onto the small space she strains to reach up while flinging the jeans only to lose her footing with her arms flailing to keep her balance. They fail to do the job and she tumbles to the floor.

The good news is being 5-foot-nothing means it isn't a long drop. The bad news is that she grabbed hold of one of Daniel's shirts *enroute* pulling it off its hangers.

Sitting in a heap of overturned laundry basket and blue jeans with her hands full of flannel shirt Milly starts to giggle. She buries her face in the soft material, trying to stifle the sound, but instead sniffs deeply.

"Why are you in my room?" yells an incredulous Daniel. "And why are you sitting on the floor and what are you... is that my shirt? and are you... smelling it?"

Muttering *caught in the act!* to herself Milly tries to scramble upright but her leg is twisted under her body. She isn't hurt but is deeply embarrassed and clumsy in her haste to get up and get out of Daniel's bedroom.

"No, I fell, I lost my balance and grabbed your shirt on the way down, I was trying to put away your jeans! but I'm just too short."

Milly is practically in tears she's so frustrated at the predicament she's created for herself, and indignant at Daniel's expression that's both angry and disbelieving.

"I'm sorry, okay? It was an accident." Her voice chokes on the last phrase and the emotion leaves Daniel's face as he smooths his features.

Reaching out to help her up he says: "I think you're just the right size," and immediately looks surprised at his own remark.

Ignoring the outstretched hand Milly tries once again to get upright but instead crumples and rolls like an armadillo. Or how an armadillo would roll if it was tangled in a faded plaid shirt. She wants to howl in exasperation but is speechless when Daniel breaks out in a huge belly laugh. He laughs long and loud and an astonished Milly finds herself unable to control her own explosive laughter.

It's only nervousness! she tells herself but thinking that doesn't make it any easier to get under control. She knows she looks a sight sprawled on the floor half-wrapped in Daniel's clothes with the two of them hooting and chortling with glee.

Their noise has drawn both Esther and Samuel who stand goggling at them from the doorway. *Oh this is so embarrassing,* thinks Milly ruefully. Herself lying among scattered laundry and Daniel bent double he's laughing so hard. To add to the slapstick comedy Bernie comes tearing into the room and races around adding his excited barks.

Between gasps and giggles Daniel and Milly finally manage to tell the tale. Samuel helps Milly to her feet and Esther picks up the empty laundry basket just as Hannah comes storming through yelling at everyone to quit messing around with her clean laundry, and why is that dratted dog upstairs?

"Hannah you're back already?" gasps Milly, stifling her laugh.

"I saw the time and called Joseph Michaelson to tell him to stay open for me 'cause I was on my way when he says my husband had come by more than an hour ago. Why Jim didn't phone me to say he got his stuff I don't know but he'll be getting an earful when I get home. Now, all of you clear out and let me get on with this."

"Oh no Hannah, I'll do it—"

Spearing Milly with a gimlet eye Hannah declares: "You've done quite enough Milly, thank you very much."

Daniels fails miserably to cover up his new laughing fit and Milly snorts in her attempt which sets Esther shrieking *you're a snort laugher!* and everyone – with the notable exception of Hannah – is off again in gales of mirth.

Milly is delighted to see this side to Daniel, and a good hearty laugh does them all good. Chastened under the irate housekeeper's eye they all hurry from the room.

Hours later, when Daniel is tossing the day's clothes in his hamper the memory of Milly with her face deep in the folds of his shirt comes to mind and the image stays with him long after he's gone to bed and is trying to sleep.

Puppy Love

Over the next couple of days Milly develops a lifelong case of *puppy love* while she and Bernie become fast friends. Daniel is busy covering Amos's chores as well as his own so she volunteers to take the puppy for his first check-up with the vet.

Since Luisa was Nora's Maid-of-Honor Milly met her at the wedding but Luisa didn't stay long so the two never really had a chance to talk. Today she acknowledges Milly with a quick smile but is all business as she inspects Bernie from head to tail.

The moment the Milly led Bernie into the clinic, with it's mixed scents of animal, disinfectant, and pee, the puppy balked and whined. Between Hannah's prodding, Kate, the receptionist, cooing over him and Dr. Bautista's professional handling Bernie soon calmed down. Now he's licking everyone and everything that comes within the orbit of his mouth.

Once the exam is finished and note-taking completed the vet indulges in a few minutes of playtime. Milly is at the desk picking up a bag of supplies Daniel ordered and being told today's bill will be added to the Young's Farm monthly account.

Seeing how excited Bernie is Milly hustles him out the door before he can pee inside. He holds it in until they're well away from the front door and Milly kisses his head telling him he's *such a good boy!* the manic wagging of his tail shows he fully agrees.

"Yeah well you better not mess in my car, buster!" warns Hannah.

Returning from their appointment Milly takes Bernie for a walk in the berry fields. She's careful to keep him on his leash because even though he's still a puppy he weighs more than fifty pounds. A rambunctious dog that size can wreak havoc on tender plants.

Spying his master up ahead Bernie strains at the leash and Milly struggles to hang on.

"You can let him go," calls Daniel and Milly is relieved to drop the leash. Bernie races to greet him joyously.

"I was hoping to see you, Daniel, I figured you'd want to hear what Dr Luisa has to say about this fellow."

Bending to hold Bernie's face close so he can scratch under his chin Daniel asks the dog: "Were you a good boy for the Doc?" Bernie vigorously wags his tale and Milly confirms he was very well-behaved and took his shots with minimal fuss.

"That's him all vaccinated up to his first year. At 12 to 16 months he'll need more. His ears, mouth, teeth, eyes, heart, coat, foot-pads – everything is exactly as it should be. The vet's exact words were *he's a fine healthy specimen.*"

The two of them are looking at the dog with admiration as Milly gives the report. Bernie is busy sniffing the ground, the plants, the stones in the pathway... deeply intent on his quest – whatever that might be – with his tail slowly sweeping back-and-forth.

Daniel speaks in an easy, relaxed voice and Milly realizes it's been a long time since she's heard this tone from him. He smiles at her saying: "Thank you for taking him. With Amos away I don't have as much free time so I appreciate it."

"Daniel it was truly my pleasure. I've never had a pet, well there were parrots at the home but I didn't like them. They're mean and they bit hard. Whenever they were let loose from their cages I made sure to be in another room. But Bernie, he's a real pet, and I'll take him to the vet or anywhere whenever you like."

Looking at the dog she says: "Can I be your dog-sitter, Bernie? Would you like that?" Bernie barks a reply as if he understands Milly's words. She stoops down to grab the end of his leash explaining that she wasn't sure if he was allowed to roam freely in the fields.

"He shouldn't. He doesn't understand and will cut straight across a row of fruit bushes if something or someone catches his attention. He's fine off-leash in the orchards. The only thing he'll do there is pee on as many trees as he can manage! That won't hurt those trees."

"I'm looking forward to getting apples this fall for baking and making applesauce and chutney—"

Daniel interest is piqued. "You make apple chutney? Yourself?"

"Sure I make a good one that's both sweet and tangy."

"I think we've only ever had store-bought."

"No, really? Well I'll be sure to put up some after the harvest. I've been meaning to ask: the berries you grow are available all summer, right?"

"Yes, we grow berries year round," pointing he directs her attention to the far side across two fields of plants. "See those shelters over there?"

"Those white structures in canvas or plastic or something?"

"Yeah, we call them high tunnels, but some farmers say hoop houses."

"Actually you could call them hoop tunnels, they look like a combination of those names."

Daniel surprises both Milly and Bernie with a loud laugh. He doesn't explain but smiling goes on to explain that the high tunnels protect the crops from bad weather and hungry insects. Both of them converse in a relaxed friendly manner because he enjoys talking about his work and she is genuinely interested.

"By bad weather do you mean storms, like hail-storms? or frost?"

"Frost in the winter, definitely at the end of December, and thunder storms in the spring that can bring hail, but the tunnels provide a safe environment for our plants."

"Am I allowed to go over there and look inside? or are the tunnels off-limits?"

"I can show you around," begins Daniel before abruptly changing his tone to add "but not today or for the next while, I'm just too busy right now."

Milly ignores the scowl he's now wearing and giving him her sweet smile simply comments that she *looks forward to it when he has the time.* Then she turns away and gently tugging Bernie's leash calls over her shoulder "I think this boy must be desperate for a drink of water so we'll say goodbye. C'mon Bernie."

Daniel stays watching the young woman with the frolicking dog walk back to the farmhouse long after the frown fades from his face. Milly would have been reassured if she's only known.

The Grand Tour

Daniel doesn't make Milly wait long for her farm tour but he does insist Bernie stay home. Hannah complains that the dog gets underfoot in the kitchen so his food and water bowls are kept in the boot-room where they've made him a bed with a few chew toys for his entertainment.

Daniel is all-business but friendly enough as he leads her to watch the workers busy with their routines. Trucks are driven on the paths into the fields so the pickers can pack their fruit directly into plastic cases with the Sweet Berry Cove logo prominently displayed. The containers get weighed and put in cardboard flats, again showing the colorful branding of the co-op.

Milly sees how Daniel's workers greet him with smiles as business news is exchanged and personal pleasantries shared. She thinks it's a good sign that the farm employees are so open and relaxed with their boss.

She gets a few curious, furtive glances until she introduces herself as the new employee at the Young Family's Farm Shop telling them: "I get to sell your lovely produce, and the goods we bake using it, but honestly it sells itself. Everything always looks scrumptious!"

Hearing her heartfelt praise and knowing she isn't a family friend of the owner but another worker like themselves relaxes everyone. Milly has a dozen questions and they're all keen to answer with lots of good-natured teasing, boasting, and sampling of the fruit. Daniel grins at the easy camaraderie being shared.

Moving on to the next field he talks about irrigation, sprayers, and groundwater use but Milly finds the technical speech boring. Catching her trying to cover up a yawn Daniel jokingly asks: "So should I skip that part of the talk that deals with transplanters, straw spreaders, and rototilling?"

"Oh sorry," she smiles revealing two deep dimples in her round cheeks. "I know water is a very important and serious subject in California but I don't really understand why when we've got all of the ocean right beside us. I mean, can't they just remove the salt and use it?"

"Unfortunately it's not that easy. A lot of special interest groups are involved – and rightly so – but the result is the State keeps rejecting proposals to build desalination plants."

"Why? what are the objections?"

"There are concerns about the effect on marine life when the ecosystem is disrupted, and worries about pollution from the discharge. People often forget that the ocean is a living thing and there are consequences to every action."

"Oh I see, and yes... you're right. That sort of thing does stir up strong feeling. Daniel, it's good to hear from someone so well-informed and interested in their work."

He brushes off her compliment but he's smiling. Milly feels emboldened to probe further.

"You know Daniel, the way you speak sometimes it makes me wonder.. um, I don't know what you think but ... but I guess I should just ask you straight out." Daniel's body draws away from her and he has a wary look in his eye.

"Tell me truthfully, do you think I stole that money?"

His obvious surprise, followed by relief, at her question makes Milly wonder what he thought she was going to ask him.

"What I think isn't important, all that matters is Dad believes you're innocent and the Young family will all do everything we can to help you."

She gazes deeply into his eyes before candidly answering: "What you think is important to me, Daniel."

His reaction shows in widening eyes and dilated pupils. Briefly overwhelmed by emotion his response is a harsh rejection when he hisses: "It shouldn't be, because I don't think about you or the theft at all. I mean, it doesn't make sense that you would take the cash from the safe but I don't know you, do I? I really can't say what you would or wouldn't do." He's scowling now, irritated and annoyed.

Milly bites down on her lip to keep it from trembling. Assuming a bright and carefree tone she replies: "That's all right then. It sounds like you're keeping an open mind which is all I can ask for. You'll decide about me when you're ready."

Turning away to continue their walk through the field she misses his puzzled look, as though he was expecting her to say something quite different for the second time now.

That evening, while a balmy breeze wafts a floral scent through the air, Milly sighs contentedly commenting: "It's nice sitting here on the porch after dinner each evening but what do you do – where do you go – when the weather turns cold?" Rocking lightly in her chair she asks the question of anyone interested in answering.

It's Samuel who responds explaining: "Actually we only made a habit of gathering out here this particular summer. Because there were so many of us in the house this year. In wintertime we keep a fire going in the family room so everyone gravitates there.

Of course Esther usually sticks to her room to do homework but we all suspect it's really to chat and text with friends while surfing the Internet – doing all three things at once!" He's grinning as he casts a sidelong look at his daughter who rolls her eyes and exhales a weighty sigh before she gets up and goes inside.

"I'm sure I'll be glad of the cozy warmth once winter arrives but for now I'm glad we can still enjoy this mild evening air."

Daniel hasn't said anything but he's sitting contentedly and following the speakers with his eyes. When Milly turns towards him he's never looking her way, but if she glances sideways she can see his gaze lingering on her.

"So Daniel gave you *the grand tour* today and now you're an expert on Young's Farm, right?"

Milly laughs and turning to Daniel says: "You were a great tour guide but..."

He smiles back. Although he doesn't have his father's unshakable certainty that Milly is innocent of the theft, a lifetime of faith in his parent reassures him. He can sit here enjoying their company without having to take a stand or make a declaration.

"I saw Milly's eyes glaze over when I explained how the sandy and clay mix of our soil means we can grow all types of fruits, like how strawberries do better in sandy loam soils and–"

"Poor Milly!" interrupts Samuel. "You should have told her the interesting stuff like all the fruit festivals that Sweet Berry Cove Farming Cooperative is involved in."

Swiveling to face Milly he continues: "It's a big deal for folks round here and the visitors who come, too. Different fruits are featured depending on the time of year. Strawberry festivals are particularly popular in May, but we have festivals for every season."

"Is all the selling done through the co-op?"

"All the fruit selling, yes, but people can rent booths to sell related goods. Like, um... help me out here, Daniel."

"Well there's that family who sell the soap they make by hand. It's shaped like fruit and smells like it too."

"That's right! and Esther got all excited about buying some earrings at another booth where all the jewelry was fruit-themed, remember?"

"Oh that is interesting," murmurs Milly her eyes losing focus as her mind is occupied.

"Interesting...?" prompts Samuel but Milly puts him off replying: "An idea but it needs a lot more thought before sharing."

"Well I have faith in your ideas, Milly, because the Farm Shop's online store is doing a great business. Better than we anticipated, that's for sure."

Even Daniel nods in agreement as they discuss which products are proving most popular so far. Samuel is impressed commenting that Milly *has all the facts and figures at her fingertips.* She blushes prettily at the praise and confides that she did have another idea but then catches herself and stops abruptly.

"Don't hold back, Milly. You're obviously excited and it's great that you're thinking up improvements to the business."

"Yeah, what's this idea you've got?" asks Daniel, his gruff voice isn't particularly welcoming but he is looking directly at her for a change.

Milly pushes down her excitement and after a pause and a deep breath tells them: "I noticed that when the locals drop in at the Farm Shop they tend to hang around for a while. They chit-chat with each other while checking out our food display so I thought, what about offering – selling, I mean – a single slice of pie and a cup of coffee or a glass of fruit juice?

There's room for a couple of cafe tables and chairs and if we needed more we could set up a couple outside..." Her voice trails off waiting for a response.

Looking at his son Samuel demands: "Daniel, why didn't we think of this ourselves?"

Chuckling Daniel replies: "I guess 'cause before Milly came to work in the Farm Shop nobody ever hung around."

Milly's eyes are bright and her cheeks pink with pleasure at their warm reception to her proposal.

"I could be a waitress!" cries Esther, "and I bet I'd make tips, too!" The three of them turn to the house seeing Esther on the other side of the screen-door. Milly thinks it's odd that Esther just stood there listening but teenagers are unpredictable.

"I realize you probably won't do anything until Amos and Nora get back but in the meantime we could work out what we'll need and get a rough estimate of costs."

Smiling at her Samuel says: "Milly, Nora doesn't run the Farm Shop. She's only been helping us with the web-store during her summer vacation. She's taking the Fall semester off but will be back teaching full-time come January. So you'll be the one in charge.

Of course we want you to discuss any ideas with us first because change has to be introduced gradually here or people will object to *incomers with fancy ways*. But please, draw up a plan showing what you'll need to make this work and what kind of prices you'll be charging to make it pay."

"Oh, I'll need help with that. I used an existing budget for the spreadsheets at the foster home so I didn't have to figure out anything new..."

"Well if you get started I'm sure Daniel can answer your questions and maybe even put in a suggestion or two."

Milly's face shines with pleasure as she asks: "Would you really help me, Daniel?" Daniel is nodding *yes* though his mind is trying to find an excuse to say *no*.

The look Samuel bestows on the two young people is positively gleeful.

An Unappreciated Savior

"There's a tasty sight for you, Milly."

Hannah gestures out the window over the sink and when Milly joins her she has a good view of Daniel splitting wood. He's stripped down to his undershirt and she can clearly see the muscles bulging in his forearms and biceps as he performs the swinging and chopping motion like a choreographed dance.

A hot blush covers Milly's cheeks at Hannah's teasing remark. She quickly turns away but not before noticing a sheen of sweat sparkling on his skin which makes her question *why is he doing such strenuous work on a hot sunny day? Even Bernie is sprawled out napping.*

Hannah explains: "When apple trees die it's best to get the wood cut and stacked as soon as you can in order to let it season for as long as possible. The wood he's chopping now will serve us well on chilly Spring nights."

"Not until Spring? what about this winter?"

"Oh the wood we'll be using come wintertime is already drying. As I said, apple wood needs lots of time but it sure is worth it."

Seeing Hannah smile over a memory Milly asks: "Why? does it burn better or something?"

"If you have to ask it means you've never smelled an apple wood fire so you're in for a treat once the cold weather sets in," the older woman assures her. "Anyhow, much as I enjoy watching a fit man work like a well-oiled machine I've got grocery shopping to do so I'm off. You don't want to change your mind and let me buy some croissants?"

"No thanks, homemade croissants taste so much better."

"But it's hours and hours of work," Hannah needlessly reminds her.

"Easy work, though." Hannah shrugs her shoulders and leaves Milly to get on with it. Once the older woman is gone Milly returns her attention to the work-table where she's rolling and folding her dough.

After working steadily for about half an hour Milly is startled by a sharp cry piercing the air. Knowing it has to be Daniel she runs out to the yard and finds him clutching his arm with blood flowing freely through fingers. Without missing a step Milly spins around and races back to the kitchen to grab a couple of towels.

She has to dodge around Bernie who is dancing around in agitation. Daniel's jaw is rigid and he's panting through clenched teeth. Milly has to pry loose his fingers to get the towel wrapped in place and then pulls it as tight as she can. Pushing his hand back down on the covered wound his ragged hiss tells her how much pain he's in.

"That's got to be stitched up, you need the doctor," she says calling the emergency number programmed into her phone and switches to speaker so Daniel can hear too. They listen to Doctor Watkin's message stating he's *at East Ridge farm and won't be available for hours.*

Daniel's face falls at the news and he groans: "That means Annie Stephenson's in labor. They've been expecting it will be bad and that's why Doc's had to go instead of just the midwife." He staggers over to sit down on the stump where he's been chopping and trembles with the movement. His whole body shakes as a shiver runs through him.

Bernie tries to jump in his lap, anxious and whining at the sight and smell of Daniel's blood. Milly tries to grab hold of the dog's collar but he snaps at her and she pulls back, knowing the animal is fearful. Daniel roughly admonishes: "Bernie! Down!" and the dog crouches at his feet.

"Good boy," Milly tells him then turning back to Daniel continues: "The shock is making you cold, hang on and we'll get your shirt on you. Here it is," she says picking it up.

Daniel tries to sit straight as she slides the sleeve over his hand and pulls the fabric up his arm. It sticks since his skin is damp with sweat and she has to tug at it. Reaching his shoulder she pulls the fabric across his back as best she can, hooking it around his other shoulder and loosely tying the empty sleeve to hold it in place.

Milly is very aware of how close the two of them are but thinks Daniel is too chilled with the tremors to notice since all he says is: "Doc's been on his own all summer, there's no one else."

"But you can't just wait. What about an ambulance to the hospital?"

"Huh! What hospital? We're no where near one here in the Cove and it has to be a real emergency to get one from SLO."

"This is a real emergency!" cried Milly, but Daniel is already shaking his head.

"But what are you going to do, Daniel? What can I do for you?"

"Can you find me some glue? there must be some in the kitchen somewhere. Some of that will work."

"What? No! *Krazy Glue* is a crazy idea it will... I know!" Milly cries excitedly, "Dr Bautista. When Hannah drove me there with Bernie the other day Dr. Bautista mentioned she has so many patients staying over that she'll be stuck hanging around the clinic for several days."

He gives her an incredulous look asking: "You seriously want me to go get my arm sewn up by the vet?"

"Yes! Why not? It's better than bleeding to death waiting for hours."

Daniel thinks it over then ungraciously snaps: "Fine. I'll go. Let's see... yeah my truck keys will be on the hook by the kitchen door."

"Okay, I'll get them."

"Don't worry about it, I've got to go out that way anyhow so I'll–"

Milly interrupts with a shocked declaration: "You can't drive!"

Daniel shrugs: "I have to."

"No, you can't. You'll just be a hazard to yourself and everyone else on the road. I'll drive."

"You can't drive."

Yes I can, I've been driving for years."

"Then why don't you have a car?" he questions her like he's just scored a point.

Looking at him sitting there with his free hand clenched in a fist and his colorless face grimacing in pain Milly gives a strangled cry of frustration exclaiming: "Why am I standing here answering your silly questions? C'mon, we've got to get going right now."

"No, I want to know why you don't own a car."

Exasperated Milly chooses to humor him because the sooner she can get Daniel into his truck the better. "I'm saving up to buy a car but I don't have enough money yet. There, satisfied? Now let's go."

She's tugging on his good arm to get him moving. "You must have plenty of money now," Daniel says and Milly releases her hold on him like she's been burned. From the look of shocked hurt on her face that's exactly how she feels.

Daniel almost apologizes but instead presses his lips tight together to keep the words back. Milly gives a tight nod as if confirming something to herself. Standing straight she simply repeats, "We've got to go now."

"Can't you call someone? Dad had a meeting in SLO today but where's Hannah?"

"She told me she was going grocery shopping but I don't know if that means the village or if she's gone into town. It doesn't matter though, there's no time to lose."

"Look, the only vehicle here right now is mine and it's that old standard-shift pick-up out at the horse barn."

Walking to the barn Milly calls over her shoulder: "That's fine, I can drive stick."

"You?"

Blowing out a frustrated breath Milly says: "Yes, me. What's so surprising about that? C'mon, Daniel do you need help? if not, hurry up."

"Hmmph, well maybe... but the gears stick and slip and you'll never manage."

"I'll be careful. Maybe I won't manage well but you won't manage at all. So let's stop arguing and get going."

The first time Milly saw Daniel's ancient truck she was amazed it still ran. Remembering that now she feels uneasy but reminds herself there's no choice. She has to get Daniel to the clinic and since that means driving the old beast then that's all there is to it.

By now Daniel's normally ruddy complexion has gone from white to gray and the towel is sopping with his blood. Every minute counts.

Being parked in the barn has sheltered the truck from the sun's glare but it's still very hot and stuffy inside. While Daniel struggles to get himself settled in the passenger seat Milly rolls down the windows. Bernie joins them for the ride and Milly sees Daniel's shoulders sag with relief once they're on their way.

That doesn't prevent him from grumbling and griping the whole time, starting with a complaint because she used the horse mounting block to get up in the driver's seat. Milly wisely holds her tongue.

After repeating instructions like *ease it in*, and just *jiggle it a bit* Daniel relaxes when they finally get onto the main road and no shifting is required. As they near the first turn he warns her to start pulling on that steering wheel now and she needs all her strength to swing it round.

Continuing on another straight stretch Millie comments: "Good thing it's your right arm well, not good but you know what I mean."

"Why do you say that?"

"Because you're left-handed, right?"

"Right?"

She can't help a giggle escaping. "I mean *yes*. You're left-handed, yes?"

"I am but how do you know? I don't remember ever writing anything in front of you."

"No you haven't, or if you did I didn't notice, but you wear your watch on your right wrist."

"So you figure that's the only way I can buckle it on?"

"No, I figure that's to stop it from getting all scratched up when you are writing something."

"Hmmph, I don't even know why I still wear a watch. I've always got my phone on me so I don't need one. Look, you don't need to talk to distract me or something, maybe you should just concentrate on the road?"

Ignoring his snark Milly states: "It's a nice watch, was it a gift?"

"Actually yeah, from my parents on my 21st birthday but... really just from my mom. She was always in charge of buying us our birthday and Christmas presents because my father isn't the sentimental type."

"Maybe not, but he's very kind."

"I expect most men treat you kindly, Milly," Daniel remarks with a sneer.

She thanks him and smiles before turning her attention back to the side road leading to the veterinary clinic and misses his speculative frown.

Milly seems to accept what I said as a genuine compliment, he thinks, *but how could she?*

"Doctor Bautista are you available for a.. a... well, a patient, so-to-speak," asks Kate, uncharacteristically hesitant as she hovers at the door to Luisa's office. The doctor raises an eyebrow at her receptionist, sure she'll get the whole story later.

"I saw Daniel's ancient pick-up creep its way into the yard so sure if the Young's have a patient for me bring it right in."

Kate steps back and Luisa hears Daniel's voice stating: "I don't have a patient for you, I have me," as he marches stiffly through the door.

Daniel's got his forearm held up with a blood-soaked towel wrapped tightly around it. The new employee at the farm shop comes in behind him then quietly steps to the side of the room.

Luisa is surprised that such a pretty girl is so shy and self-effacing but then she remembers the accusation going around. *Still just a rumor though*, she reminds herself, her thoughts unconsciously siding with the young woman against the spiteful gossips of the village.

As a Latina Luisa knows how it feels to be an outsider in Sweet Berry Cove but she wryly acknowledges the huge chip she had on her shoulder, and her readiness to challenge anyone who looked sideways at her, when she first came here.

This girl has a completely different nature. Much softer, more easy-going... she wracks her brain to remember her name. She didn't mention it when she brought Bernie in for his first check-up. Luisa knows that Nora used it when she spoke of her temporary room-mate and then of course they met during that awful primping session before the wedding... *Milly!* Luisa remembers triumphantly.

"Good of you to bring Daniel in, Milly," she says smiling to herself when Daniel scowls and Milly blushes. Continuing she teases: "Especially since you seem to be an unappreciated savior."

"I can wait for Doc Watkins, he's at East Ridge farm with Mrs. Stephenson who's having a difficult birth, but she insisted on driving here to bother you," he grumbles ungratefully.

"Ah that explains the cautious driving. Daniel normally races around in that miserable old truck spewing exhaust fumes everywhere."

Unrolling a paper liner over the table Luisa says to Daniel, "After all the kids Annie Stephenson has had if Doc thinks there's a problem now I expect he'll be gone for hours," before turning back to Milly to add: "So it's just as well you brought him in before he loses any more blood."

For a moment Milly's trademark shy smile appears but a frowning glance from Daniel wipes all trace of it from her face. Luisa stores up that little by-play to gossip about with Kate after her visitors leave.

Daniel balks at sitting on the examining table but Luisa pushes him down complaining: "You're just too tall for me to deal with so perch here and let me have a look at this arm. What were you doing, anyhow?"

"Chopping firewood."

The vet just stares at him with her mouth hanging open in shock. "How the heck did you cut your right arm chopping firewood? If you'd cut your foot or even took off a toe or two... but your arm?"

"I was distracted, I guess," he sulks with embarrassment pressing his lips tightly together ending further conversation.

Normally that wouldn't stop Luisa but before she can ask the obvious she makes an exasperated sound asking why on earth he's left Bernie out in the truck barking his fool head off.

At Daniel's succinct *no leash* explanation Luisa hollers out to Kate to *fetch a leash and drag that noisy mongrel inside.*

While they listen to the frantic scrabbling of claws on a tiled floor Luisa unwraps the ruined towel. By time the excited puppy pulls Kate into the room the vet has exposed the deep gash in Daniel's arm.

"I usually have to sedate my patients before suturing up a bad cut but you'll be able to stay awake for this, right? I mean you won't bite me, will you Daniel?" she teases.

The big man looks comical when he rolls his eyes and mumbles *I might* while his dog struggles to climb his master's legs. Giving up on that idea Bernie then decides to dart between the women bumping them. Milly drops down to her knees to quiet the dog, patiently accepting the sloppy wet kisses he's licking all over her face and throat.

Luisa and Kate exchange a knowing glance after they both spot the softening of Daniel's expression as he looks on. They also see him harden his gaze when Milly looks up and catches his eye. Kate quietly tut-tuts, returning to her desk out front, and Luisa concentrates on sewing up Daniel's wound.

He grunted a little before the topical numbing solution took effect but now looks on with interest at the straight line of neat stitches. Luisa dabs at the few drops of blood that well up then slathers an antibiotic ointment over the whole area before bandaging it in gauze.

She finishes getting Daniel into his shirt and considers buttoning it for him but instead a wicked impulse has her asking Milly if she can please help out.

"It's fine, I can do it," insists the stubborn man. The two women watch his fumbling and Luisa doesn't even bother to hide her grin.

Without a glance or a word Milly reaches forward and deftly does up the buttons before returning her attention to the dog, but not before both Daniel and Luisa see her lips twitch over a repressed smile.

"Keep an eye open for any spreading redness or, of course, oozing pus, and make sure you don't get it wet in the shower," instructs Luisa back in professional mode again.

Snagging the bloody towel with the table covering she shoves both into the big garbage receptacle. "Oh! I can wash that," says Milly but Luisa just shakes her head answering: "Daniel can afford to buy another one."

He huffs out a "Huh! If you think I'm so rich I'm almost afraid to ask how much I owe you?"

"No charge," Luisa replies. "I'll get a kick out of sharing the news of my latest patient with anyone who is interested. Oh wait! this is a small-minded little village where everyone is always interested in everything. I'll spread it around."

Stopping on his way out of the examining room Daniel turns back saying: "There are plenty of good people in this town, Luisa."

Acknowledging this the vet says: "I know there are. Kate's one, I'm another, you're another, and so is Milly." Her face wears a serious look but Daniel doesn't respond to her remark.

"As you pointed out I can afford to pay so I'd like to square up with you."

Luisa just shakes her head at him. He grudgingly says: "Thanks for the freebie, then," shouldering open the door for Milly and Bernie to precede him before heading straight to the driver's side of his truck.

The girl whispers a thank you while grabbing hold of the dog's collar to unhook and return the leash. Eager to leave the vet's clinic, Bernie drags her to the truck and jumps inside through the driver's door.

Giving an impatient sigh Daniel hoists Milly one-handed around her waist until she's perched in the high driver's seat. Slamming the door he stomps around to the passenger side where he's enthusiastically welcomed by a flurry of brown and white fur and floppy ears.

Milly can be seen heaving on the big steering-wheel as she backs the truck out of its parking space and points them out of yard. The gears grind noisily as usual.

"That must be a difficult vehicle to drive," comments Kate.

"Well yeah, it doesn't have power steering or power brakes, and just a manual transmission, and–"

"And a miserable passenger giving the directions," interrupts Kate with a laugh.

"For that girl's sake I hope the painkiller kicks in to mellow his grouchy self."

After a nerve-wracking drive back to the farmhouse Milly thankfully parks and switches the old pick-up off. Jumping down she hurries around to the passenger side. Daniel has already opened the door but it's obvious his strength is failing. Either than or the painkiller has kicked in, Milly isn't sure which.

She swings the door wide and grabbing hold of his good arm starts pulling him out. Bernie is darting about between them, pausing to give a few loud barks. The dog understands that something is wrong and when he nuzzles Daniel's hand he whines at his master's lack of response.

Standing just over 6 feet tall Daniel towers over Milly by more than a foot. She wedges her body into the side of him and braces herself as he half-slides half-falls out of the truck. He doesn't try to straighten up, just hangs over her as she struggles to move him into the farmhouse.

"Daniel please, please try to walk. I'll help but there's only so much I can do."

He's woozy and unfocused as he looks down at her saying: "You're just a little thing, aren't you? But you sure are pretty, Milly."

His eyes roll and she's afraid he'll collapse so she stomps down hard on the instep of his foot. That has little impact since he's wearing tough work-boots but he feels the movement and jerking his head up sways unbalanced and uncoordinated.

Milly is ready to cry at the hopeless situation but just then Samuel comes running from the fields accompanied by a couple of farm-hands. He's got his phone to his ear and Milly hears him shout "Yes, yes they're here now. Thanks for calling to warn us, Luisa."

The three men lift Daniel off of Milly who falls back against the side of the truck trembling. Samuel steadies her while the workers each take one of Daniel's arms over their shoulders and do their best to walk, but mostly drag, the injured man.

"Go around to the kitchen door," calls Samuel after they've hesitated, daunted, by the front porch steps.

"Come on, Milly. We'll get Daniel settled in the front parlor for now and Hannah will get a hot drink into you. You've had a shock. I'm so glad I came straight back here after my meeting in the city.

Luisa phoned when she realized you'd have trouble moving Daniel once you got him home. Taking him to her was quick-thinking on your part and I thank you for looking after my boy."

Looking at Samuel Milly sees he's more formally dressed then usual, even wearing a bolo tie, and remembers he had something on in SLO today. She can't remember what, her mind is a bit fuzzy. Without realizing how she's giving herself away Milly dismisses Samuel's gratitude by saying: "Oh I'd do anything for Daniel."

Hours later, while lying in her bed, Milly groans remembering what she said. She regrets speaking her thoughts out loud while Samuel was listening but acknowledges the truth of the words.

But I have to bury those thoughts and never mention them again, she tells herself. *Just like I have to stop thinking about Daniel telling me I'm pretty...*

Next day State Trooper Merkel returns with his superior, effectively glossing over any concerns about improper thoughts being remembered.

No Femme Fatale

When State Trooper Merkel and his superior officer, Deputy Superintendent Poole, come to interview Milly the next morning the Young men are still at the breakfast table. The two of them insist on remaining at her side while the police ask their questions.

Faced with this evidence of the injured party's support Officer Poole acknowledges to himself that the case against his chief suspect is shaky. Still, now that he's come out here he'd like to finish the job and move on.

"Ms. Clarke I'd like your permission to search your room for the missing money."

Daniel opens his mouth but Poole forestalls his question stating: "I don't have a warrant, this is an informal search just to make a note in the file stating that it was done and frankly Miss, it's for your benefit, too."

"Yes sir, I see your point. I just... well, it feels," she hunches her shoulders indicating her discomfort and glances over at Samuel who gives her an encouraging look saying: "I'll go and watch over them, Milly." So she nods.

The three men leave and, surprisingly, Daniel takes hold of Milly's hand. To do so he has to shift around awkwardly, stretching across his bandaged right arm. He doesn't say anything, just sits quietly with his big hand enclosing her much smaller one in warmth. She's grateful but too wrapped up in the embarrassment of policemen rummaging through her belongings – even her most personal items – to say anything.

It's only a matter of minutes before the tromping sound of boots on the stairs reaches them as the men return to the dining-room. Daniel smoothly releases Milly's hand by standing up and moving to the door to direct them out. Deputy Superintendent Poole thanks Milly for her co-operation while the young trooper just ducks his head in a nod.

Without speaking to anyone Milly busies herself in the kitchen. Her whole body sags in relief when she hears the trooper's car pull away.

A moment later Hannah comes in asking: "What on earth was Robbie Poole doing here? Not still bothering you Milly, I hope? I guess I'm not surprised though, we were at school together and he was a few sandwiches short of a picnic back then and I don't imagine he's changed much since. Honestly, these men..." shaking her head she opens up the closet of cleaning supplies to grab her basket of polish and rags and gets to work.

Despite the delay in setting out Milly heads for the village walking slowly. She's in no hurry to complete the task she's set for herself. Now that she understands how deeply she cares for Daniel she realizes she can no longer allow any other men to waste their time or affection pursuing her affection. It isn't fair on them.

She hopes she can hang on to the friendships she's enjoyed but isn't sure how that will work out. It's a shame because these people have stood up for her against the accusations of stealing. They've proven to be true, loyal friends.

She's never really had friends before. At the home young people came in and out of her life sporadically. She'd had a few crushes, but in secret. The foster home was a temporary dumping ground rather than a long-term solution for most of the kids. Except for Milly who did all her growing up in the home. She never learned how to make and keep lasting relationships but she wants to honor the friendships she's formed here.

Although she believes wholeheartedly that honesty is essential she isn't looking forward to the conversations. Not that she's going to make a big deal out of it because she's never been a fan of supersized emotions and drama.

The Sweet Berry Cove Library is actually part of the Sweet Berry Cove Elementary School. The library is accessed from outside the building but visitors can walk through into the school itself. Under the watchful eyes of one of the Harrigan sisters, the librarians, that is.

After renewing her library book for another two weeks *of course you've been far too busy to finish it,* and a pleasant rehashing of the wedding ceremony Milly says she's just going to pop in to see the school principal.

This deeply interests the Miss Harrigan she's been speaking to, and every step of her progress is monitored. Milly fights the temptation to turn around at the door and give a little wave.

Based on pretty much every conversation she's ever had with Peter Showalty she knows he'll ask her for a date. They met for the first time at Nora and Amos's wedding and he's made his interest in her very clear.

On seeing who his visitor is the man jumps up from behind his desk with a welcoming smile. Milly starts off by saying *she knows he has to be extremely busy with the school year having just begun* but he waves away her apology.

Closing the office door and ushering her to a chair Peter, true to form, asks Milly when she's going to let him take her out. She's always made excuses to avoid a dinner-date but twice they've enjoyed a takeaway coffee and a walk along the shore. Peter is a great conversationist and

Milly always has a good time in his company. But she's here now to put a stop to him asking her out again.

"Peter I value your companionship, very much, but I'm not interested in dating," states Milly with a serious look.

He sits back with a smirk on his face, ready to accept the challenge of the game, but after a moment spent studying her realizes she isn't flirting or playing hard to get. Milly means exactly what she's saying.

Deflated he asks: "Is this a *carved-in-stone* decision or can I hope you might change your mind?"

"I won't, but thank you for being charming as ever," she smiles as she gets to her feet.

There's something about Milly's calm yet firm demeanor that prevents Peter from trying to plead his case. He's disappointed, because he likes her very much, but he can tell when a young woman has made up her mind.

Although he'd dearly love to know *why or maybe who?* he's too polite to ask.

Instead he sees her to the door with the reminder: "I'll be seeing you at the school's Halloween Dance Party since you agreed to be a chaperon, right? and remember to wear a costume, too. Have you been told what this year's theme is? Oh, of course, Nora will have let you know."

"I'm looking forward to the dance, I'm sure it will be fun. Goodbye, Peter," she says holding out her hand.

Mindful that they're under the watchful eyes of both his secretary, Joanie Robson, and Verna Harrigan across in the library, Peter makes sure their handshake is friendly and brief.

Once she's cut through the library and is back on the street Milly lets loose a big sigh of relief. Her meeting with Peter went well and she believes their friendship is still intact.

Thinking of his good-looking face, always ready to break into a smile, and his bright blue eyes that show such a flattering interest in her, she feels a slight pang of regret. It would be so easy to allow herself to be loved but Milly knows Peter isn't the one for her.

She continues with her unwelcome but self-imposed chore of distancing herself from any men who might be interested in more than friendly acquaintanceship.

Going into the Post Office she had hoped for a bit of privacy when speaking with Jay but his sister, as usual, stays close by. Shrugging mentally Milly figures it's fine for Kay Somers to overhear because it's a surefire way to get the word spread.

The conversation is short with Jay's responses clipped and stilted, generating an air of embarrassment that Milly is thankful to escape.

Any other men in the village, like the guys at the garage and the volunteer firefighters, who have flirted and even asked her out, will soon hear the gossip.

Finally she walks back up the hill from the other end of Sweet Berry Cove heading for the church to see Stephen, Reverend Smithson. She sighs deeply suspecting this will be her most difficult conversation.

He really does seem smitten and as an older man his outlook is more serious. Plus, there are certain expectations of a man in his position and she must do everything she can to preserve his dignity. Milly indulges in an even deeper sigh as she nears the church. Straightening her shoulders she comforts herself with the knowledge that this is her last stop.

I'm certainly no femme fatale, she thinks. *All this attention is only because I'm new and young and single in a closed community. Obviously I was bound to attract attention, Miz Tally said as much and I enjoyed it but... I have to do the right thing.*

Stephen Smithson's delight at discovering that Milly is the person he hears walking through the cool shadows of the old church is short-lived when he sees the rueful, uncomfortable look on her face. His first concerned thought is *what's happened? what's wrong?* but then the young woman explains.

"Stephen, this is difficult for me to say but I believe you have feelings for me that go beyond mere friendship?" she doesn't give him a chance to reply before hurrying on to say, "and if I'm wrong please excuse my presumption, but if I'm right I feel it's only fair to let you know that I can't reciprocate, my heart is set on someone else."

Stephen stands very still absorbing her words and the sinking feeling they're causing him inside. He knows himself well enough to realize that he's been hoping for much more than friendship with Milly Clarke.

Looking at the pretty young woman struggling to maintain her composure he is overwhelmed with regret but also acceptance. What he desires... is not meant to be.

"You aren't wrong in what you thought, Milly, and I can't pretend I'm not disappointed. However," he gently lays his hand on her shoulder and smiling reassures her: "I appreciate your honesty, I do."

Milly's face relaxes and she lightly pats his hand before stepping away without speaking further.

A Knight in Shining Armor

Milly doesn't show up for lunch which leaves the family free to discuss the story of her breaking hearts that is making the rounds. Hannah heard it firsthand from the postmaster's sister, and Esther overheard the Harrigan sisters gossiping in the library.

Despite listening intently Daniel doesn't react or join in the speculation. Instead he pushes back from the table announcing he *ate too much and is going for a walk* but he's really going out looking for Milly. Bernie is missing so he figures she's taken the dog out for some exercise.

Wandering through the orchard the fragrant smell of the fruit trees eases his nerves until he finishes the circuit without catching sight of her. Where can she be? Heading across the field where the wildflowers are mostly dead and dying, he turns to look out at the water and spots a person marooned in the cove with the tide pulling well up the shoreline.

Realizing it's Milly he mutters to himself about *the carelessness of foolish young women.* Hands on hips he watches, waiting to see her jump into the water. She isn't wearing a bathing suit and he feels a grim satisfaction thinking that she'll struggle a bit with all her clothes on.

Of all the stupid things to do, he thinks. Milly is still on the rock and she isn't preparing to dive, instead she's pacing back and forth. She looks agitated and her body language is... suddenly he's hit hard with the thought: *Oh no! what if she can't swim?*

Fearing there's not enough time to run along to the easier pathway Daniel scrambles over the cliff-edge. His racing feet slip and slide on the tussocks until he manages to pick his way down to the water quicker than he's ever done in his life.

Bernie is at the water's edge running into the shallows then quickly back out again, barking the whole time. When he hears Daniel come crashing through the switchgrass he stands still as a sentinel directing his master towards Milly and the danger she's in.

Spotting Daniel on the shore Milly starts jumping up and down frantically waving her arms and calling *Help! Help me, please!* She doesn't stop, even after he plunges into the cold water and is swimming towards her. He realizes she's panicking in her terror.

Refusing to be distracted his mind narrows its focus to figuring out the best way to bring Milly in safely. He's certain she's too wound up to float alongside him but he's concerned that putting her on his back might mean she strangles him out of fear. He knows she isn't strong enough to actually accomplish that but her thrashing and fighting will make her swallow huge amounts of seawater. Plus he isn't at full capacity with his arm stitched up.

Daniel is a powerful, experienced swimmer who represented his school in State-level swim meets. He didn't pursue the sport past that point because qualifying for higher competitions would require too much training for a farmer's son.

Daniel has always known his future is at the family farm by duty and by choice. But he's never lost the sheer enjoyment he's always felt by being in the water until this moment. Now he understands that the swirling depths and pull of the tide can be horrifying to a non-swimmer.

Before he's properly in ear-shot he hears the pleading tone in Milly's voice as she begs him to please save her. Closing the gap he's dumbfounded when one phrase, spoken in a high-pitched tone, comes through clearly: *Daniel please, please stop hating me long enough to rescue me!*

He has to put his reaction to that comment aside because he's arrived at the part of the rock that isn't submerged. The surface is only a foot square and with no more room to pace Milly has been hopping from one foot to the other. Daniel is surprised she hasn't slid off with the way the water is washing over.

Just as he thinks that she's knocked down by a wave and slips into the water on the far side of the rock, away from him. Now Daniel feels the terror of being helpless in the ocean and gets a small taste of what Milly is experiencing.

I'm so scared, so scared, so scared... The seawater is cold, icy cold, and so incredibly salty. That wave pushed me into the depths tumbling and screaming, my mouth wide open from surprise. It's utterly pitch black here. I thought Daniel was coming for me but I guess I imagined him. This is what drowning is... freezing blackness and losing my mind. But I'm not dead, I can hear the pounding of my panicked heart-beat. My arms and legs struggle against the weight of this cold water sinking me although I know thrashing about is the worst thing I can do... But then all Milly's thoughts disappear as mindless terror sucks her under.

Daniel has the bulk of the rock to brace against as he comes round it using his strongest strokes. A whirlpool of splashing and churning water alerts him to Milly's location. Diving blindly into the maelstrom he grabs hold of her and, as expected, she fights against him.

Petite Milly has turned into a dynamo of thrusting arms and frenzied kicking. Her adrenalized strength surprises Daniel but only for a moment. Firmly wrapping one hand around her throat he pulls her head out of the water and floating on his back drags her up on top of his body.

Face to face like this her stunned look of utter horror sends a pang right to his heart. *No one should ever suffer such terrifying fear*, he thinks. *Her eyes are fixed on mine but she isn't seeing me, she's still petrified.* He gets a good tight grip on her hoping the strength of his hands will alleviate some of her dread.

Air... air!!! I can breathe again! thinks Milly as she drags in deep lungfuls.

That's the only thing she's capable of focusing on right now. She's aware that her airways hurt with each gasp of her shallow breaths and her heart is racing but her mind has no thought beyond breathing in air instead of water.

Daniel decides that turning the two of them around is too tricky so he simply holds Milly in place and kicking his legs lets the pull of the incoming tide do most of the work. He wants to crush her tight against his chest until she calms enough to realize she's safe.

In part of her mind Milly does know that Daniel has hold of her and she's safe now but she can't fully believe or acknowledge it. She's still wholly wrapped up in her panicked reaction underwater.

Floating takes longer but gives Milly the chance to finish her spluttering, gasping, cough as she brings up seawater. As soon as he can touch bottom Daniel stands and hoists Milly over his shoulder knowing she can spew the remaining seawater down his back if he holds her in this position.

With Bernie dancing between their feet Daniel carries Milly quite a ways up the beach before the two of them collapse on the sand. He pants for breath while she sobs from sheer relief and the dog barks and licks and shakes out his wet coat all over them.

The first words out of Daniel's mouth are: "Can't you swim?"

Milly drags her sodden locks back from her face and not trusting her voice yet simply shakes her head.

Daniel is harsh when he hollers: "Why not? The ocean has been right there your entire life, how come you never learned?"

The fragile grip Milly has on her composure is lost in an explosion of temper. She knows she looks awful with her hair hanging wet alongside her face and her clothes plastered to her body. She was really frightened and Daniel yelling at her makes everything worse. But the stimulus of heated anger pushes the suffocating fear deep down, grounding her, while she vents all her emotion in a loud rant:

"When would I have the time? and who was going to teach me? I grew up with nothing: dirt-poor in a commune surviving on the kindness of elderly hippies. It's not like I ever had a family, and being home-schooled with the other abandoned kids meant I never had a chance to make lasting friendships. There was always a long list of chores to be done just so we could get by and any leisure time was spent learning to cook and bake on a budget.

I was taught to drive when Benji lost his license, and I've had training on the computer, but I can't swim, I can't ride a bicycle, and I can't play any sports."

Daniel buries the guilt he's feeling under his own anger demanding: "Then what the He– heck were you thinking wading out against a rising tide?"

"Bernie was stuck on that rock, he couldn't get back!"

"This dog here? the one that's happily splashing about in the water because he's a dog so naturally he can swim?"

"But Dr Luisa said–" Milly has to cut short her explanation because her teeth won't stop chattering now that reaction has set in and her whole body feels the cold.

"The vet was talking about... oh here," Daniel breaks off to start vigorously rubbing Milly's arms and back as he explains Saint Bernard's aren't good swimmers but the puppy could manage the shallow water easily enough before the tide rushed in.

Daniel realizes that since he's soaking wet as well he can't offer her much body heat so it's best to get back to the farmhouse as soon as they possibly can. He scoops Milly in his arms and hurries to carry her home when she cries out: "But your arm!" And he assures her that she weighs nothing and saltwater won't do his stitches any harm.

Feeling her body suddenly droop he looks down at the girl he's carrying and he sees she's closed her eyes and appears to have fainted. He's concerned by a bluish tint to her lips, emphasized by her very pale skin. She feels extremely cold.

His head fills with the unwelcome thought that *she could have drowned... Milly could have died! and she would have done so thinking I hate her? where did that come from?* He pushes that thought away and scoffs at his reaction reasoning that it's normal to be concerned when someone you know is in danger.

"You did the right thing, or thought it was, which is very brave but also very, very stupid. Milly, you should never put yourself at risk like that." He has no recollection of bending down to kiss her forehead but when he draws back he's startled to see her blinking up at him. He's betrayed himself and she's caught him!

Desperate to cover up he clears his throat saying: "Just checking your temperature."

"With your lips?" Milly's own lips twitch with an unexpected smile.

"No! well, yes because my hands are kinda full. Besides, lips are very sensitive and able to sense heat and... and uh.. your skin is still cold but you weren't unconscious for long so you should be okay." The words are ridiculous and he feels like a fool.

Milly notices how tightly he's clenching his jaw and sadness fills her knowing she's angered him once again. She keeps her eyes closed for the rest of the journey home even after she hears his whispered promise of *I'll teach you how to swim.*

After learning about her ordeal Samuel insists Milly *go to bed immediately.* Hannah follows her to her room and hands over fleecy sleepwear for Milly to put on while she takes away the wet clothes to wash. Tucking the girl in to bed the housekeeper tells her she's excused from breakfast duty in the morning so she can sleep straight through.

Samuel gives Milly fifteen minutes before knocking on the door to check up on her. With the duvet pulled up to her chin only Milly's face can be seen and it's as white as the pillowcase she's lying on. Samuel shakes out the quilt folded at the foot of the bed where Nora had slept and lays it over Milly's own quilt telling her when the adrenaline rush fully subsides the subsequent shock will be chilling.

Daniel stops by but stays in the doorway. After a quick glance at Milly he tells his father *just checking on her* before turning away.

Even though it's early and still light out Milly falls asleep right away. She does sleep right through the night until her internal alarm clock wakes her up to fix breakfast. During a quick trip to the bathroom she realizes she's still bone-weary and decides to follow Hannah's advice and go back to bed.

It's mid-morning when Milly awakens fully. Throughout the day she suffers through flashbacks of the overwhelming, paralyzing fear that overtook her when she was faced with going into the water. The ensuing trauma when she actually fell in was the single most frightening occurrence of her life.

It's hours before her hands stop trembling, and she never does quite manage to shake off the shivers or the ache in her legs and arms. Bernie sticks close to her, sensing her need for comfort.

Several times she's tried to speak to Daniel but it's like he knows what she wants to say and so he manages to sidestep any mention of thanks. Yesterday's long sleep plus the frustration of not expressing her gratitude is keeping Milly awake tonight.

It feels like she's been tossing and turning for hours but Milly knows it isn't midnight yet. She's heard the big grandfather clock at the bottom of the stairs chime the eleventh hour only moments ago. The clock is set to overnight quiet mode and it won't start up again until 6:00 the following morning.

Milly just can't get comfortable. She's dragged her blanket on and off, flipped her pillow over twice, and rolled from one sleeping position to another all without success.

It's not that late, Milly reasons, *certainly not too late to go outside for a breath of fresh air.* Replacing her nightgown with shorts and a long-sleeved t-shirt she tucks her shoes under one arm and quietly opens her bedroom door. Tiptoeing out she moves down the stairs slowly, hoping to minimize the sound of creaks and squeaks common to old wooden structures.

Reaching the bottom with a sigh of relief Milly slips on her moccasins while studying the lock on the front door. It's a simple snib from the inside but a key is required to get in so she has to be careful not to get locked out.

Slipping out back through the kitchen door makes the most sense except Bernie is sleeping in the boot room and he might bark. Not wanting to cause a disturbance she eases open the front door and the screen door, steps through, then reaching back pulls it almost closed but not quite. The screen-door always snaps back with a bang so she's careful to close it gently.

Milly's shoulders slump with relaxed pleasure as a gentle and not too chilly breeze wafts over her. Tilting up her face she studies the bright moon, it was full just a week ago, and what seems like a billion stars crowding the night sky. Settling on the porch steps she once again tilts her head back to look her fill.

Daniel knew someone was moving through the hallway even before the tell-tale warning of the second-from-the-top stair-tread. Bernie, having once again sneaked out of the boot-room and found his way up on the foot of his master's bed, raises his head and gives Daniel an inquiring look. The dog already knows who's moving around and doesn't bark.

Although he's lying in bed Daniel isn't close to falling asleep yet. He's not often given to introspection but tonight Daniel follows the trail of thoughts uppermost in his mind. Thoughts about Milly and what could have happened to her, about Nora and Amos's wedding, and about how the future he'd always hazily envisioned for himself could actually become his present.

Inevitably that leads his thoughts back to Helena and he's pleasantly surprised to discover he doesn't feel the usual anger or bitterness towards the woman who betrayed him. In fact, he's now questioning whether he was truly heartbroken? or just so deeply shamed at being tossed aside in favor of another? How much of his hurt feeling was simply wounded pride?

Hearing someone creeping about is a welcome distraction from facing unwelcome truths. Dressing quickly and quietly he follows with Bernie in his arms and one hand wrapped around the dog's muzzle to keep him silent.

Pulling back the front door and half-opening the screen Daniel pauses to study the sight of Milly ahead of him sitting on the stairs. She's perched a few steps down with her back resting on a riser while she looks up at the sky.

Having her head tipped back like that makes the ends of her long hair, all auburn tinting hidden in the dark, brush the floor of the veranda. While he watches she unwraps her arms from around her knees and leans back until she's supporting her weight on her elbows. Daniel glances up to see what she's looking at and it takes him a moment to realize the sky view, although same-as-usual to him, is probably totally new to Milly.

He comes through the doorway and Milly lets her head fall right back to see who's behind her. She isn't frightened in the least knowing the person has come from the farmhouse.

"It's late to be out," he says.

"Not too late, and I'm perfectly safe here on the porch."

"True but you'd be just as safe in your bed so why are you out here?"

"I couldn't sleep so I came outside for some air and then I saw this sky. Now I understand what people mean when they talk about light pollution because I've never seen anything like this. Daniel it's... it's magnificent and stunning and it makes me feel like I'm just a speck of dust in comparison to this vast expanse."

"When you put it like that," he chuckles, "it's true, that's exactly what you are."

"Well then you are too so I don't know what you're laughing at," she answers but with a smile softening her retort. Turning serious she gives him her most imploring, wide-eyed look as she says: "Daniel, I can't begin to find the words... to express my deepest, deepest gratitude—"

He shakes his head in a dismissive way telling Milly: "I'm a strong swimmer and I reacted instinctively."

"But you saved my life, Daniel!" Adding, with a huge smile, "You're my *Knight in Shining Armor.*"

"Hardly! I'd do the same for anyone I saw in trouble in the water." *Why do I say stuff like that?* he wonders.

Bernie's wriggling is impossible to contain so Daniel sets the pup down before he falls. In a burst of speed Bernie races to Milly delighted to have her face on a level with his own so he can deliver a flurry of licks. She collapses in a fit of giggles that Bernie matches with his rapidly wagging tail.

Daniel finds himself smiling at the scene before reality comes crashing back in as he remembers the theft from the Farm Shop. He'd conveniently forgotten all about that, instead indulging in tender thoughts when he rescued Milly and held her in his arms.

Now he remembers and even though he's undecided about whether or not she did actually take the money he isn't willing to open up any further than he already has.

Stepping over the girl and dog sprawled in play he jogs down the stairs stating: "Guess I have to let this guy go have a sniff round and a pee since we're up and outside."

Milly sits up, brushing herself off, and asks: "May I join the two of you?" fully expecting a *yeah, sure* answer but is rebuffed by Daniel's casual, "No, not this time."

Worded like that it sounds like he might entertain the idea at another time but Milly knows that if he can't even be bothered to manufacture an excuse well... Bernie, torn between his two favorite humans, opts to snuggle against the one who has stiffened with hurt. Milly hugs the dog close but then releases him when Daniel whistles for his pet.

Keeping her feelings in check she responds: "I'll say good night then," and quickly lets herself back into the farmhouse.

Milly climbs back up the stairs as quietly as she came down because she doesn't want to encounter anyone else. Safely back in her room she changes into her nightie once again and slides under the covers.

I can no longer deny my feelings for Daniel, she thinks sadly. *I can't pretend I only see him as my savior, even though he literally is! I have to be honest with myself. I had feelings for Daniel long before he rescued me from drowning.*

Living through that danger has brought all kinds of feelings and truths to the surface forcing Milly to acknowledge with her mind what she already knew in her heart.

Being in love with Daniel Young is one of the truths I have to accept, she declares. A thrill of excitement ripples through her whole being. Happiness bubbles up and she revels in it, in the joy of falling in love. She wraps her arms around her pillow hugging it close and giggling into the fabric *I'm in love! I'm in love!* It doesn't matter that Daniel doesn't share her feelings it's enough, for now, for her to enjoy them.

Gently rocking herself Milly looks through the window and thinks the moonlight – this exact same moon that's shining on Daniel right now – has made her tipsy.

Her last thought before slipping into sleep is *of course I have to guard this secret and keep it hidden. I can't bear the thought of how he'd sneer if he caught me wearing my heart on my sleeve.*

Return of the Prodigal

It's a joyous occasion when the happy couple return from their extended honeymoon. The Young's are such a close family that both Amos and Nora were very much missed while they were gone. Everyone is eager to hear about their adventures on the cruise, and to pass on the news they missed here at home.

The weather is still mild so they've all gathered on the porch. Bernie is meeting these family members for the first time and they're delighted to greet the excited puppy.

"It's great to be back on solid ground after weeks on a boat. I mean, it's such a huge boat you really aren't aware you're moving on water but once you're back on land you can feel the difference. Of course I loved the cruise, every minute of it, but oh it's good to be home!" exclaims Nora.

Giving both of them a hug Samuel says: "The two of you look terrific, so relaxed and happy. Married life suits you, both of you."

"Oh I'm already a pro at being a husband, I no longer try to get Nora to call the boat a ship—"

"Amos! I know, I know but I keep forgetting and you're a sweetheart not to nag me about it." She gives him a quick peck on the cheek and the two share a secret smile.

Daniel and the ride-share driver have been ferrying luggage and shopping bags onto the porch. After paying the man Daniel asks Amos: "Where's all this going?" Before his brother can answer Nora points to two overnight cases saying: "We only need these tonight. We'll just shove the rest in the sitting room with the wedding presents and tackle everything tomorrow. Or the next day... there's no rush."

"Except for giving me my presents," Esther reminds her sister-in-law.

"It's the *return of the prodigal* son, indeed!" jokes Amos.

Laughing Nora agrees that presents are important and they've brought home plenty of souvenirs as well. She's yawning hugely and the wearying strain of travel shows in Amos's face, too. Daniel loads up and carries the various items inside while Nora leans into her husband who draws her close.

She says: "We'll each grab a case and say goodnight. Tomorrow's a big day at the school with the Halloween Dance Party."

"I'll take both cases, wife. You can get the door," Amos tells her.

"Good night Nora, good night Amos. It's so good to have you both back. I look forward to hearing all about your trip after we've all had a good night's sleep," says Samuel.

"Good night, Dad. It's great to be home again."

Everyone lingers over breakfast the next morning. The chat about village gossip is interspersed with Nora and Amos's reminisces from their cruise.

Even Daniel is lighthearted and humorous as he relates the tale of Milly driving him to the vet in his old rattletrap pick-up.

"Milly, you never!" gasps Nora.

Amos wants to speak but he can't get the words out he's laughing so hard. Finally he splutters: "She drove that decrepit old truck of yours?"

Which brings on more chuckles at the fake offended expression Daniel wears when he says "Don't make fun of Sweetie!"

"But why the vet? What did Luisa say?"

"We couldn't get Doc Watkins, he was tied up at the Stephenson farm and–"

"Oh! Annie's twins, what did she have?"

"Triplets," replies Samuel dryly.

"Wh-What? Oh wow! We knew it was a multiple birth but everyone thought twins–"

"That woman just pops them out like there's a sale on," comments Hannah coming through from the kitchen.

She doesn't normally work on a Saturday but has stopped by to help with the costumes. She enjoys getting get involved with the children's parties, but she isn't a member of the women's group from the church who are organizing the decorations and refreshments.

"Oh Hannah, what a thing to say," admonishes Samuel.

Hands on her hips the housekeeper demands: "Well how many Stephenson kids is that now?"

"Well... let's see, I guess with these three it's eight?"

"Eight, right. Eight kids in one family in this day and age. Hasn't the woman ever heard of—"

Nora quickly interrupts Hannah saying: "Just like that old TV show *Eight is Enough*, remember?"

"Anyhow, the size of the Stephenson family is their business and Hannah for all your grumbling I'm quite sure you've already been by to do laundry and lend a hand."

"Oh pfft, someone has to help out."

"And the babies?" asks Milly.

"Two boys and a girl, all healthy if the pitch of their hollers is anything to go by. They're small but darn cute," she concedes.

"I'm so glad, that's really good news," remarks Nora.

"Yeah, you never have to worry about getting laid off from your teaching job so long as the Stephenson family is here to keep your classroom filled up," teases Amos.

"Oh sure go ahead and laugh at me. I thought we were laughing at Daniel going to the vet to get his arm sewn up? I can't wait to ask Luisa about it."

"Well you'll have to wait because we've got to get started on sorting out your costumes. You've been sitting over the breakfast table until lunchtime!"

They all go to their rooms to get dressed up then meet again to show off their outfits.

Since it's a K-8 school the festivities start and end early. Plenty of adults will be there to assist and supervise and, as they do every year, they'll dress to a common theme.

This year they've chosen the medical profession in honor of the hard work and sacrifice workers made during the Covid-19 pandemic. The inhabitants of Sweet Berry Cove were fortunate, no loss of life, but most people knew someone living elsewhere who'd gotten sick.

The children can choose to wear whatever costumes they like so there will be plenty of Disney Princesses and Marvel Superheroes as well as the usual witches, hockey players, and clowns.

All the local teens are invited to the dance so Esther is attending too. She liked the idea of painting her face in Zombie make-up but wants to look like one of the adults so she's going as a Nurse.

Hannah cleverly constructs a nurse's cap from a white envelope and attaches it to Esther's hair with many admonishments to *keep your head still or those bobby pins will go flying*. It's decorated with a red cross and matched with a plain white dress and white sneakers the girl does look the part.

Nora and Amos go as Paramedics. Their costumes are actually matching navy cotton pajamas worn with toy stethoscopes, part of a collection Nora borrowed from her students back in the summer when the theme was settled on. They've stuck a big red cross on the hood of the SUV so it will look like the family is arriving in an ambulance.

Samuel is wearing a white jacket he's dug out of his closet along with a children's toy stethoscope, head mirror, and doctor's bag. Milly has on a pink-and-white striped summer dress transformed into a *Candy Striper's* uniform with the pinafore Hannah provides along with a big pink bow for her hair.

"You look like Dorothy from *The Wizard of Oz*," says Esther.

Milly grins at her before loudly belting out the opening lines of *Somewhere Over the Rainbow* in a beautiful singing voice. She's always held back her ability during the hymns at church so her audience is left open-mouthed in surprise. Milly curtsies at their applause.

She and Samuel are escorting Daniel, their patient, who has a bandage wrapped around his head and is wearing a dressing-gown and slippers, and leaning on Samuel's fancy silver-topped walking cane. He fusses over having to dress up at all but not-so-secretly enjoys the annual Halloween party.

"I was wondering how you all celebrate Halloween since the farms are too far apart for kids to be out trick-or-treating," comments Milly.

Nora explains: "On the 31st the children wear their costumes to school for a little party. We let them out an hour early so they can go into the village where all the merchants hand out candy–"

"Except the dentist," complains Esther. "She gives tiny tubes of toothpaste and a couple of pieces of sugar-free gum."

"Growing up there was always a party at home and we took turns with our neighbors on each side to see who would host it," puts in Hannah. "Once we got a local school the party was switched to there."

"I didn't realize you grew up here too, Hannah," says Milly.

"Hmm, yes I was raised on a farm but I'm very happy with my little bungalow and my non-farming husband."

"Hannah's Jim is a diesel mechanic so there's plenty of work for him here in Sweet Berry Cove," adds Samuel.

After the costumes are given final tweaks the Young family and Milly pose for photos that Hannah takes with her phone. "I'm not switching around from one of your phones to the other trying to figure them all out, I'll just send these from mine to each of you."

They all cram into the vehicle except Hannah who will drive down with her husband. Everyone is in happy anticipation of a fun event. They can hear the K-Pop music blaring as soon as they enter the school.

Festive orange-and-black streamers decorate the hallway leading to the gym where games like bobbing for apples are being played by the younger children, and there's a story time circle for the very youngest. The older kids make a beeline for the dance-floor, and there's a pumpkin-carving competition for all ages. Every attendee will take home a little bag of Halloween goodies.

The chaperons have their hands full helping little ones to the bathroom, rounding up straying teenagers from the hallways, and applying band-aids when necessary. At one point Daniel spies Milly sitting cross-legged on the floor re-tying the sash on a very small girl's party dress into a big bow. Milly says something to her and the tears on the child's face quickly dry up as she flings her arms around Milly's neck.

Looking over the girl's shoulder Milly catches Daniel's eye on her and she's held in a spell, basking in the warmth of his gaze. All his harsh words and accusations are forgotten in that one splendid moment. Soon enough other people walk between them, breaking the connection, but Milly clasps that happy feeling to her heart and locks it in her memory.

A photographer is busy taking photos for both the school's archives and the church's circular. Soon a parade of children will form so everyone can admire the outfits and some will win ribbons for having the funniest, prettiest, silliest, and most creative homemade costumes.

The meal is a corn roast, grilled hotdogs, and a variety of ice cream flavors for dessert. Most of the young families will leave after they've eaten.

The lights are slightly dimmed and a DJ plays dance tunes. Hannah and Jim wow the crowd with their two-stepping performance. Milly dances with Peter Showalty and Stephen Smithson. She is disappointed that Jay Somers has chosen to give her the cold shoulder, but is delighted when old Mr. Sullivan asks her to honor him by taking a turn round the dance-floor.

Daniel gets out of taking his turn by pointing to his cane but Samuel is quick to take his place. Later every single person gets up on the dance-floor for a tarantella that has them all spinning from arm to arm as the tempo goes faster and faster.

Afterwards, laughing and gasping for breath, Daniel complains: "I shouldn't have been dragged out on the floor in my condition–"

Perplexed, Milly reminds him: "But Daniel, your foot injury is just a fake, remember?"

"Oh that's right! That means... that means I can do this," and he grabs Milly by the waist and twirls her around until she's dizzy.

Her smile is so wide her cheeks are dimpled and her eyes are shining when he holds her close until she regains her balance. Before the moment can deepen into something meaningful it's broken by Esther's cry of: "Daniel, spin me now! It's my turn."

Nora and Amos have been dancing a slow dance no matter what song is playing. Wrapped up with her head resting against his chest and his arms around her waist it's obvious they are newlyweds deeply in love.

The lights come up and the partygoers gather their belongings and call their *goodnights* as they head out. The ladies of the church get busy packing up the leftover food while their husbands are set to bagging the trash. A volunteer group has already been arranged to meet next day for clean-up.

All the happy faces are testament to another successful Sweet Berry Cove Annual Halloween Party and Dance.

Unmistakable Ring of Truth

It's a friendly, convivial atmosphere during the church service this Sunday. *They're all feeling good about last night's party,* thinks Milly, relieved at the change. *Or maybe it's because we're here in full force today.*

That was true, with the exception of Samuel all of the Young family was in attendance and sitting together in their regular pew. The churchgoers were happy to see Amos and Nora and when Reverend Smithson welcomed them back home plenty looked over to send smiles and friendly nods their way.

After the service there's lots of handshaking and socializing on the church steps. It's only that Janice Peart who tries to discuss the theft from the Young Family's Farm Shop but she's effectively quieted by the combined efforts of Milly and Miz Tally who prevent her from causing trouble.

Esther has gone off with a couple of girlfriends to dissect their observations from last night's dance so it's just the four adults walking back to the farmhouse.

"Milly are you cold? or am I just feeling it more after being away in the tropics?"

Taking Nora's arm Milly assures her: "It's not just you Nora, it is chilly this morning." The two women are walking side-by-side just a few steps ahead of the brothers.

"I promise to warm you up once we're back home, sweetheart," Amos calls out with an exaggerated leer. Nora doesn't answer him but when she leans close to whisper something in Milly's ear, causing the younger woman to giggle, Amos can't hide his grin.

Eager to return to a neutral subject Daniel comments: "The weather forecast is calling for near-frost conditions later this week and that feels about right."

"One thing I like about the change of seasons is putting away the outfits I'm tired of and getting out last year's favorites to wear again."

"I like that, too! Milly, we should go into SLO and browse the boutiques to find one new thing each."

"Nora, that does sound like fun. I haven't left Sweet Berry Cove since I arrived and.. and maybe we could have lunch and eat seafood?"

"Oh poor Milly, it sounds like you've heard all about Hannah's aversion to fish dishes?"

"I guess you had plenty of seafood on your cruise?"

Amos joins the conversation saying: "Milly they fed us so well with a real huge variety of food."

"That's true, both of us gained a few pounds, didn't we Amos?"

"Luckily there was a gym on board and I managed to get some time on the treadmill to burn off calories. Everything was cooked to perfection–"

"And beautifully presented, too."

Laughing Daniel says: "Stop! you're making me hungry and we're only halfway home."

"Okay, we'll walk faster just for you Daniel," teases Nora. She does pick up the pace and tugs on Milly's arm to pull her along. "We're better off going into SLO on a week day but we better not mention it in front of Esther or she'll want to cut class to join us."

"I guess if you're born in Sweet Berry Cove a trip to town is a big deal."

"And going shopping and lunching, yeah."

"Do you want me to drive you, hon?"

"No thanks, Amos. This is strictly a girls-only outing."

Hannah didn't cook the lunch today since she and Jim are coming over in the evening for a visit to hear all about the honeymoon cruise. Instead, Milly left a homemade soup simmering while they were at church and Samuel now complains that he's been sniffing the tantalizing aroma for hours and thought they'd never get back.

The five of them sit down to a casual meal of soup and fresh-baked bread with an apple pie for dessert. Afterwards Nora declares it's time to clean out the front room and Milly helps her put away the wedding presents and open their luggage to sort out gifts, souvenirs, and laundry.

"I should get started on a wash–"

"Don't be silly," interrupts Milly, "You know Hannah enjoys doing it and will be expecting plenty to keep her busy. In fact, just getting this room cleared out will make her happy. She confided to me that she hasn't been able to vacuum properly for weeks."

"Oh I can just imagine!" answers Nora chuckling. She's piling the soiled clothing back into the suitcases to make it easier to carry.

Lifting packages to check underneath and behind Milly turns to Nora with a puzzled look asking: "What happened to all the cards you'll need for your thank you notes?"

"Oh, I took them with me–"

Nonplussed Milly exclaims: "On your honeymoon?"

"Yes, I wrote them during our days at sea. I bought postcards which gave me just enough room to say *thank you for the whatever and we're having a lovely time.*"

"What a great idea! That's so clever."

The two women continue working and make great headway. Nora fetches Amos to help carry the suitcases to the laundry room. Milly suggests the boxed wedding gifts can be moved to the spare bed in her room until their final destination is determined and Nora greets the idea with enthusiasm.

Daniel is corralled into lending a hand carrying the stuff upstairs and finding himself alone in Milly bedroom he takes the opportunity to look around at her things. She hasn't added much, just a silver-framed wedding photo that looks like it's of her parents, her hairbrush, and some perfume bottles. When Milly joins him with another armful of gifts he suddenly feels self-conscious being in her space but she's blithely unaware of any awkwardness.

They soon have the front room restored to normal and can relax for a lazy day. The five of them chit-chat about events in Sweet Berry Cove over the past couple of months but whenever the talk veers to the Farm Shop Milly sidesteps questions by stating the web-store has taken off brilliantly and they'll go over everything when they open up tomorrow.

The women listen to the men discuss co-op news for awhile before setting out a cold meal for their light dinner. Esther returns in time to eat and regale them with gossip from the Halloween party. Apparently there was plenty of intrigue among the teen element and the adults find themselves stifling smiles at the drama.

Milly decides everyone can serve themselves buffet-style from the dessert selection she's prepared so they don't need to carry trays of food outside.

"After all, the wasps that are still around at this time of year will be very hungry."

"And their stingers will be full of poison," says Samuel, approving the plan to keep most of the food indoors.

Esther and Nora join in to help lay out the coffee mugs and fixings. Hannah and Jim arrive soon after and once everyone gets their refreshments sorted they move out to the front porch.

Nora follows a few minutes later with the gifts she and Amos brought back. Everything from clothing to a boomerang that Bernie seems to think belongs to him!

Milly immediately puts in the abalone shell hair-combs she's been given and blushes when Daniel tells her she *should always wear her hair back like that instead of hiding her pretty face*. There's a surprised silence at his words which Samuel smooths over by remarking that the ornaments contrast beautifully with Milly's auburn hair.

Just then Amos jumps up to dig his wallet out of his pocket exclaiming: "Daniel I completely forgot but you must have settled up with our driver on Friday night so How much was it? I'll give you the money now so I don't forget again."

"Don't worry about it, Amos."

"I'm not worried I've got plenty on me, we barely touched the cash we took out of the shop safe on the Friday before–" he suddenly stops speaking, alerted by the stillness of his audience.

Looking at each of their startled faces he says: "What? What's up? Did I say something...?" and trails off uncertainly.

Nora is also on the alert and her tone is sharp when she asks: "What going on?"

187

Samuel catches Daniel's eye and the two host a silent conversation before he says: "You took the money that was in the Farm Shop safe? All of it?"

"Pretty much, I mean I paid the caterer's bill which was huge, and was going to buy traveler's checks with the rest, but we never got around to it, did we hon?"

"No, we didn't need much money on the ship but... it's obvious something's up, what is it?"

Daniel speaks and his voice is harsh and bitter as he says: "We thought we'd been robbed. The state police are involved in an investigation into the theft."

Amos half-shouts: "What? Why?" just as Nora turns to Esther saying: "But you knew we took the money, Esther, you were there! We told you to tell... wait, the police were called? Who do they think...oh no, oh no!" she cries realizing they're all looking from Esther to Milly who sits silent, white-faced with shock.

"Esther!" thunders Samuel, startling them all. His daughter jumps to feet, eyes darting from one face to another before she bursts into noisy tears. Her speech is practically incoherent as she gasps between sobs *I didn't mean it, I never thought the police would be involved and... and once they were I didn't know how to fix things.*

"Oh Esther," says Hannah. The girl flings herself into the housekeeper's arms, hiding her face away from the anger she sees in the men and the confusion in Nora. She can't bring herself to look Milly in the eye.

Hannah looks at Samuel who is rubbing his hand over his mouth. He nods at her to take his semi-hysterical daughter inside. Catching her husband's eye they exchange a silent communication before Jim nods and unobtrusively slips away.

"Milly... oh Milly I don't know where to begin. I am so, so sorry," apologizes Samuel.

She meets his gaze and he can see she's struggling to hold back her tears. Tears of relief now that her fears are lifted, of release since she's been vindicated, and of shock at Esther's duplicity.

Daniel is looking at her too but neither of them are anxious to make eye contact with each other. He can't help but recall the sadness he heard in Mily's voice when she told him from the start that *the truth would come out*.

He feels angry, frustrated, and... inadequate. He feels like he failed Milly and should beg her forgiveness but... should he? Before he can say or do anything Milly abruptly gets up and turns away from them saying she's going for a walk.

"I'm coming with you," declares Nora but Milly stops her firmly, requesting some private time.

"Take Bernie," says Daniel and Milly does look at him then, just a fleeting glance, but with a flash of gratitude at his suggestion. All the yelling has driven the dog to huddle under Daniel's legs. When he gets pushed towards Milly he happily follows her.

The remaining four look at each other and Amos let's out a deep sigh apologizing for the trouble he's somehow caused.

"No, no Amos and you too, Nora. Certainly neither of you are at fault. I realize I've been sitting here making excuses for Esther in my mind but at the same time I'm berating myself for spoiling her. Ever since Ruth passed... I just, I made a mess of things."

"No Dad, we're not doing this. We can't be pointing fingers or worrying about what we've done wrong, not when we have to start making things right. I'll phone that trooper, Merkel, and call off the investigation. I'm sure there will be paperwork, statements, whatever. At least we weren't the ones who reported a crime."

"Then who did?"

"This won't surprise you, it was that Janice Peart, busybody that she is. Oh that gives me an idea. Dad, can you call Stephen Smithson and tell him to notify the Church ladies to spread the word."

"Some folk will suspect we're covering up–" begins Samuel but Daniel interrupts his father saying he'll make sure the police are seen by the villagers.

"And what are you going to do about Milly?" demands Nora. "I can just imagine some of the things that have been said."

She is heartsick at the thought of what Milly probably went through but when she turns to Daniel her angry look softens at seeing the expression on his face.

"I guess we'll turn in, then. We can get things sorted out tomorrow."

"Good night Nora, good night Amos. I'm sorry your homecoming turned out this way but the good news is we don't have to give you the bad news of a theft anymore," says Samuel with a halfhearted chuckle. He stands as well and looks at Daniel.

"I'll wait," he says and Samuel, understanding, gives him a nod then heads indoors.

Darkness seems to drop down quickly as Daniel sits in silence, straining to hear the jingle of Bernie's dog tags.

After hurrying away from the farmhouse Milly drops her pace to a slow walk. Her brain feels divided in two: one side holding a mass of conflicting thoughts swirling around too quickly to grab hold and make sense of, the other half a numbing haze of blankness. She chooses to dwell in the empty space where at least it's quiet.

Bernie's natural instinct is to run around sniffing and exploring but the puppy keeps running back to nudge her shins and lick at her ankles. The dog senses her disquiet and is using distraction as a comfort.

Giving the animal a rueful smile Milly says out loud: "You're gonna cheer me up despite myself, eh pup? Well Bernie your heart's in the right place."

Bernie suddenly bounds away just as a man's voice calls out from the gathering dusk: "They say talking to yourself is a sign of insanity, Milly."

"I'm talking to the dog," Milly replies, relaxing when she realizes the newcomer is Stephen Smithson.

"Who, I'm sure replies in his own way," rejoins the reverend, bending down to scratch behind Bernie's ears. Turning his head to look up at Millie he tells her that he just had a call on his mobile from Samuel.

"Ah, so you know what's happened."

"I do and it's such a relief to have that nasty cloud of suspicion lifted at last. Mysteries are all very well on the TV but not so much in real life."

Straightening up to face her he continues: "I was cutting through the fields, heading home, when Samuel called. I told him I wasn't far away and could come over but he said almost everyone had already turned in. Instead he asked if I could just keep an eye out for you, that you were out walking on your own."

"I just had to get away for a bit and leave the family to do well, whatever it is that families do. That's something I don't know much about," she says curtly. Sighing, she adds "I wanted to think but I can't, my thoughts are all a jumble."

Stephen stops and taking hold of both her hands says: "Milly, I am deeply ashamed of my community for the mean-spirited gossip that was being passed around. I hated the thought that a thief lived among us and couldn't for the life of me figure out who it could possibly be. See, I never believed it was you yet I couldn't believe it of anyone else either. And I was right!"

"I don't blame anyone for thinking what they thought, Stephen. I mean there were only so many of us who could have taken the money and... well I am the stranger. Since I knew I wasn't the thief I..." Milly pauses and takes a deep breath, her face showing she's about to reveal something unpleasant.

"I suspected Esther. I couldn't think of a reason, I mean she's well taken care of to the point of being a little spoiled even, but when I considered who had access and who was here between Thursday night and Monday morning well... it narrowed the possibilities.

So at first I thought it must have been Esther but her denial had the unmistakable ring of truth. And of course that's because it was true, Esther didn't steal the money, and no one really suspected her.

Stephen, actually can I talk to you as Reverend Smithson, right now?" He nods but doesn't speak. Even though it's gotten quite dark now she can see his face clearly enough and his expression shows he's receptive and willing to listen.

"From the moment I learned the truth it felt like a... a blackness, not darkness but a nasty, bitter blackness running through my veins. Boiling hot then freezing cold and I was so angry – angrier than I've ever been in my whole life. And it was overwhelming! consuming me and poisoning me. I just sat there frozen yet simmering, crazy I know.

But I realized if I opened my mouth vile hateful words would spew forth at that girl for what she put me through and yet she is just a girl, just a stupid teenager with all the mixed-up feelings and emotions that teenagers suffer through. I knew I would hate myself if I said cruel things, things that maybe we could never forget... Still, I felt like I was about to lose control and had to get away."

"Oh my dear, righteous anger burns with a cleansing fire and you're certainly entitled to feel this way after the ordeal you've been through. Look Milly, I'm not going to make excuses for Esther and neither should you. By law she's practically an adult and she must apologize and take responsibility for her actions."

"She can apologize to her family but as for me? I just want to put the whole thing behind me. Stephen, thank you for letting me get all that out, holding everything in made me feel ill. I know now why Wrath is a deadly sin!"

"The aftermath of strong emotion is usually draining and you've got the right attitude about moving on from this. Milly thank you for trusting me enough to confide your feelings, and I thank the Good Lord that there's no awkwardness between us so that I can help you in this small way."

Impulsively Milly gives Stephen a quick hug just as Bernie's bark alerts them to another's presence. Daniel silently steps forward, his face a mask, but Stephen greets him without a trace of self-consciousness.

"Daniel, perfect! I know you'll see Milly safely home. And Milly, I will speak to Esther about making amends and–"

"Oh no, that's not necessary–" but he interrupts quite firmly stating *it is necessary for Esther's own sake.*

"Otherwise she won't be able to move forward herself, her guilt will weigh her down. I have an idea which I'll discuss with her and we'll work something out. Meanwhile, I'll continue on my way and, again, I'm so pleased the truth has come out at last. Such a blessing! Good night to both of you."

Bernie follows the reverend until Daniel's sharp whistle brings the dog running back. He looks at his two favorite people and cocking his head seems to be asking them a question. Milly can't help but smile and looking up she catches Daniel looking not at the dog but at her.

"Milly, I... uh," he clears his throat but before he can continue Milly lightly pats his arm and suggests it's time to head home, they can talk tomorrow. In the light of the rising moon she's seen an expression of incredible discomfort on his face and she knows she just can't deal with one more thing. Not tonight.

Turning she steps too quickly and stumbles a bit. Daniel takes hold of her upper arm to steady her and pulls her into his side keeping her close for the entirety of their walk home.

As they reach the farmhouse Milly breaks the silence musing: "I wonder why we never thought, not for one moment, that there might have been an innocent explanation all along?"

A Tall Tale

Next morning Milly has slept past her usual time but she did her breakfast prep before going to bed so the meal will be served on schedule.

She sees a couple of drawers in Nora's dresser aren't fully closed, evidence that her erstwhile roommate has come in and made an effort to be as quiet as possible. Milly smiles at her friend's consideration, especially after the long sleepless hours she spent lying in bed thinking last night.

Getting up she goes into the washroom and is pleased to discover her eyes aren't the least bit red although there are shadows underneath. Deciding the course of action she settled on in the wee hours is standing up to the light of day, Milly draws in a deep breath and prepares to face the family.

It's a bit anti-climactic to enter the kitchen and find it empty.

Usually Daniel is there after his early-morning jog with Bernie darting from the boot room, noisily lapping up water, to the kitchen where he casts hopeful hungry looks at Milly. There's no sign of man or beast this morning.

Chuckling to herself Milly is glad she decided to make a celebratory breakfast welcoming Nora and Amos home. Last night she got all the fixings for French toast ready and is happily humming when Amos and Samuel come in closely followed by Nora.

"Something smells great!"

"Is that French toast? Oh Milly! please tell me it is!" exclaims Nora.

"Oh this is a first for us, Milly. Hannah will complain that we're spoiled rotten getting *a fancy restaurant breakfast.*"

"I want to give the newlyweds a warm welcome home. We'll be back to cereal and toast tomorrow," Milly laughs.

No mention is made of the two missing family members, Daniel and Esther, as the four adults enjoy their special breakfast along with a couple of funny stories of breakfasts on the honeymoon cruise.

With just minutes to spare before the school-bus will arrive at the bottom of the lane Esther comes flying out, calling through the dining-room door *I'm late, good bye!*

Quick as flash Milly races after her and catches hold of the girl while she's still in the kitchen. Since the door's left open everyone can hear what is said.

"Esther, a moment please!"

"I don't have time–"

"Please, just listen. We'll talk later but for now I want you to know that you and I," here Milly gestures between the two of them, "we're good. There are some things to work out but we will because, well, that's what friends do."

The teen's startled expression and staring eyes show how unexpected Milly's words are but as Esther's face crumples on the verge of tears Milly simply turns back calling over her shoulder: "You better hurry, Esther. I can hear the bus coming."

Returning to her chair at the dining-table Milly is met by three varying looks: Samuel is grateful, Amos is speculative, and Nora is teary-eyed with happy emotion. Milly explains that she freely forgives Esther, easily understanding the girl's worry, anxiety, and maybe a bit of jealousy.

"She wanted to make a little trouble for me and give herself some excitement but events snowballed and then she was trapped in her lie. I don't envy her the bad nights she must have had wrestling with her conscience."

Samuel says: "That's very generous of you, my dear."

Milly waves off his compliment. "I have an idea," she tells them and they all greet this statement with interest.

"When I was in high-school I had to read some pretty boring books, well, the stories were good but the writing was..."

Amos asks: "You mean like Shakespeare? I could never wrap my head around his words."

"No, but that's something like what I mean. What I'm thinking of is the novels we studied like *The Scarlet Letter* and *Tess of the d'Urbervilles*–"

"Oh and *Wuthering Heights* and *Pride and Prejudice*," adds Nora.

"Yes and I was thinking about what happened to that letter in *Tess* and that gave me the idea to tell people that you left us a note in the safe about the money, a note that got pushed under one of those canvas deposit bags and wasn't discovered."

"But we told Esther, she was there."

"No one outside of us knows that though, do they?"

The other three think silently on this.

"But surely you've made a deposit in all this time," asks Amos.

"Actually we closed the Farm Shop to the public and have done all the business online."

"What? Why did you... oh! things were that bad, were they?"

"It got ugly - we even had graffiti - and the way I felt? I wouldn't even sell wormy fruit to any of those busybody troublemakers," huffs Samuel.

Nora pats his arm saying: "You don't have any wormy fruit to sell. Everything off your farm is pristine. But Milly, I am sorry to hear about what happened. It must have been just dreadful for you."

"Actually one of your fans came and championed us, that funny little man from the wedding, I think you have his granddaughter in your class?"

"Oh you mean old Jackson Sullivan? I saw him dancing with you on Saturday. And yes, I teach their Emmy, but what happened?"

"He tore a strip off the gossip-mongers saying something about him *falling for their nasty talk once before but never again.* He even quoted Scripture! Miz Tally arrived a moment later heartily supporting him and between them they cleared everybody out of the shop.

I was grateful, but sorry Esther had to witness her neighbors at their very worst."

"Oh, I can't help but feel responsible for all this I mean if we'd never taken the money–" says Nora just as Amos explains: "I just was so busy trying to get as much done as possible before leaving that I never made it to the bank."

"You have every right to take the money and no reason to think there would be a problem," Samuel tells them. "The whole thing is an all-round unfortunate incident... well, no. It's more than just unfortunate. Esther deliberately did wrong by keeping quiet."

"Samuel, I agree, I'm not trying to excuse what she did but... I think everything just got out of hand. If that Janice Peart–"

"Oh Milly you're calling her that too!" Nora bursts out with a grin.

"Yes, well if *that* Janice Peart hadn't been there then the police wouldn't have been called or Samuel would have been the one to suggest such a course of action and I believe Esther would have confessed to you before things went that far."

Samuel smiles at her, nodding in agreement. "I think you're right and I truly appreciate what you said to my daughter just before she left. I'm sure she's gone off to school easier in her mind and with a much lighter heart. Now this suggestion is a great idea but... well it's just a tall tale, isn't it? and us spreading it around somehow doesn't sit right with me."

"Oh Samuel I think it's the perfect solution!" puts in Nora.

"Honey, would you say that if it was one of your students and not your sister-in-law?" asks her husband. Nora purses her lips and gives her husband a rueful look. They both know she'd want her pupil to own up and do the right thing no matter what the consequences. She shouldn't treat Esther differently just because the girl is family.

"I'd like to have a chat with Stephen first. In fact, I think I'll head over to see him right now. Amos, why don't you take your bride and open up the Farm Shop. If people pry just talk about your cruise."

"We can offer to show photos from my phone, that should put them off!" laughs Nora.

"Okay Dad, we'll go hold the fort until Milly comes over and then I'll hey, where's Daniel?"

The four of them just look at each other and shrug.

"I haven't see him today but he's got Bernie with him," states Milly. That seems to reassure the others and after thanking her for the delicious breakfast they go their separate ways.

Biding His Time

Milly is sitting with her coffee in the kitchen when Hannah arrives. The housekeeper is still indignant on the younger woman's behalf but Milly sits her down and pouring out a cup for the older woman explains what she's been thinking.

"I felt so much better after I unloaded on Reverend Smithson, poor man! and lying in bed last night I turned everything over in my mind. You know, at Sunshine's foster home a lot of the kids were what's called *Young Offenders*–"

Interrupting with a snort Hannah declares: "They were just *Juvenile Delinquents*, plain and simple back in my day."

Milly pauses to think that appellation is neither plain nor simple but she doesn't want to start an argument.

"Hmm, yes, anyhow... back at the foster home in every case, every single case, the trouble these kids got themselves into was always because they did something stupid on impulse. Typical teenager actions and reactions. I really can't fault Esther.

As I said to Samuel I'm sure things went way, way further than she ever imagined and having kept silent she didn't know how to fix it when things got out of hand."

"That's a good Christian attitude you've got Milly, despite how you've been raised."

Hannah misses the surprised look on Milly's face at that comment. The woman is deep in her own train of thought, finally saying: "We've all been guilty of spoiling Esther. First she's that much younger than the boys and the only girl so naturally... and when Ruth died well... I think it's natural to spoil a young girl just like we spoil that dratted dog. By the way where is he? I usually can't keep him out of here."

"He's out with Daniel but I don't think either of them have had any breakfast so I guess Daniel lost track of time."

"Oh well, they'll turn up when they're hungry," states the housekeeper pragmatically.

"Oh! That reminds me, Hannah do we need to prepare any treats for tomorrow night? I mean, will be get any trick-or-treaters coming by?"

"No, almost definitely not but there's a good chance some adults will stop by. They don't need candy though, just a slice of cake or pie."

"Okay, good because I was thinking I could do some pumpkin tarts, peanut brittle, and caramel candy apples. What doesn't get eaten I'll take into the Farm Shop and give it away as samples. Maybe get some orders for Thanksgiving or even Christmas."

Shaking her head but in approval, not censure, Hannah comments: "You're always thinking of good things for the Young Family's Farm Shop and for the family to eat, Milly. All the hard work you put in has certainly been noticed and appreciated."

Milly waves off Hannah's compliment but she's obviously pleased at the older woman's kind words.

The two of them work on their respective chores with Hannah calling from the front room that she's delighted Nora finally got those wedding presents and suitcases sorted out so she can give the place a proper cleaning.

Milly smiles listening to the house-proud woman and is just about to answer when an unusual sound intrudes on her thoughts. Straining to hear she realizes it's a very excitable Bernie barking frantically. With a strong sense of urgency Milly runs out of the kitchen, checking that her phone's in her pocket and hollering *something's wrong!*

By time Hannah gets to the kitchen door she sees the girl flying over the field and then hears the frenzied sound of a panicking dog.

Milly comes racing into the paddock heedless of the big snorting bull once she spies Daniel lying on the ground with his eyes closed.

Foregoing his usual morning run Daniel took Bernie on a long ramble trying to sort things out in his mind. Thinking about the theft-that-never-was, and realizing he'd treated Milly unfairly, he's too wrapped up in his thoughts to pay attention to where his feet have taken him.

While his mind is occupied he climbs over one fence after the other until he's wanders into George's field. The bull is not pleased at the intrusion and comes charging, a fact Daniel only becomes aware of at the last second. He twists his body down and away, narrowly missing a goring from George's horns but he does get trampled as the enraged animal passes by.

The terrified puppy bravely keeps George from coming close again, holding the old bull at bay while barking to alert everyone that his master is in danger.

When Milly arrives she waves her arms in the air and shrieks at George who retreats from her screams and Bernie's shrill barks. She calls Samuel who arrives in a hurry shortly after with a couple of farm workers who drive the bull to the far end of the field where he paces angrily.

Amos and Nora quickly follow and she's overcome remembering her fear after Amos was attacked by the very same animal.

Amos pulls his frightened wife close when she gasps: "That horrible, evil creature has just been biding his time until he could get revenge against Daniel!"

Milly has dropped to her knees to cradle Daniel's head in her lap. Bernie snuggles against Milly while keeping his eyes glued to Daniel's face. She hugs the dog close and lets him lick her silent, salty tears as she strokes Daniel's forehead and in a soothing voice assures him everything will be just fine. She doesn't know if she's reassuring the man or the animal... probably both.

She has no idea how long she remains in this trance-like state, murmuring comfort and praying steadily, before the ambulance comes to whisk Daniel away to the hospital in San Luis Obispo.

There he receives medication, x-rays, scans, and treatment, and will fully recover.

"Knock, knock," says Stephen Smithson rapping lightly on Daniel's open door the next day. The patient holds a finger to his lips before nodding his head towards Milly curled up on a chair sound asleep.

"Ah!" says Stephen with a smile before settling in the second visitor's chair and asking Daniel in a low-pitched voice: "So, how are you doing?"

He notices that despite the grayness of Daniel's complexion the man looks peaceful and relaxed. *Well*, he amends silently, *as relaxed as someone can be lying in a hospital bed with their wrist in a cast and their leg suspended to ease a fractured ankle.*

"Surprisingly okay, actually," replies Daniel speaking barely above a whisper.

Stephen turns to look at Milly again and comments: "I don't think us talking is going to wake her, she looks right out of it."

Gruffly Daniel admits that though he's tried to get Milly to go home and rest she insisted on staying at his side, and the fondness in his gaze belies his tone of voice.

"Hmm, maybe she feels obligated to see this through since she's the one who found you, or at least that's what I heard?"

"That's right. I guess Bernie was barking hysterically and so loud that Milly could hear him from the farmhouse. She said she immediately knew from the dog's distress that something was wrong and came out in a rush.

See, she thought it was Bernie who was injured and she told me she got such a shock to find that it was me lying on the ground and that brave little puppy was running back and forth to protect me. When she added her shouts to Bernie's barking old George decided he'd had enough and retreated and then the men came and drove him back.

Milly discovered her phone doesn't have 9-1-1 access so she called Samuel who got hold of Amos and Doc Watkins... oh! I just remembered.. the doctor made some crack about *maybe he should bring in Dr. Bautista for a consultation*...huh!"

Stephen is puzzled by that comment asking: "Why would he consult with the vet?"

"Oh, that's a story for another day but I'll be talking to Doc Watkins, the sarcastic old so-and-so!" Daniel pauses, frowning over his thoughts, before his face clears and he proudly adds: "Milly climbed in the ambulance with me, she refused to leave me on my own."

"Yes, I was with Samuel when he got her call and I've never seen a man's face drain of color the way his did. Of course we all assumed you've been gored."

"Luckily just trampled. Huh! that's quite sentence, isn't it?" Daniel grimaces from the pain when he starts to chuckle. "But truly I was lucky. A bull that size could have caused serious internal injuries but all I've got are the two breaks and some pretty spectacular bruises over tender organs."

Noticing how the patient's eyelids droop Stephen stands up to go. Before leaving he gives Daniel a blessing, finishing with the sincere wish that Daniel will be back home soon.

With a final look at the girl, still sleeping soundly, he grins and waves goodbye. He realizes that Daniel is the lucky man who holds Milly's heart and he's able to feel glad for the two of them.

A Fairy Godmother

After days of much cooler weather the temperature rose enough today that when Miz Tally comes by to deliver a strawberry-rhubarb pie *just for Daniel to help him recover* she finds the family sitting on the porch.

She'd already seen Nora and Amos when they came to her home to deliver a present from their travels and tell her all about their cruise.

They'd also confided the truth about the money missing from the safe knowing Miz Tally wouldn't gossip and was also shrewd enough to see through any tales.

"We both feel so sorry and so angry about the way Milly's been treated, I wish we could make it up to her somehow."

"I have a little idea about that," says the old lady. "There are one or two things to look into but... yes, I'm going to drop by for a visit."

Now she's come to the farmhouse with the dual purpose of a treat for the invalid and a little bit of investigation for herself.

She begins by teasing Daniel, asking if he *had a premonition he'd end up in a foot cast and that's why he wore the Halloween costume of a patient? or simply enjoyed the attention so much he decided to make it permanent?*

"And to think you look like such a nice old lady, all fluffy and friendly..." he replies, adding: "Just for that I won't let you to sign my cast."

"Daniel no one can sign your cast," complains Esther in an aggrieved voice. She's been feeling out of sorts lately, uncomfortable with everyone knowing how she kept quiet about the money, even though they're all being okay about it.

"True, but it's the principle of the thing. Actually this fiberglass construction with all the nice soft padding inside is quite comfortable. It hardly weighs anything. I'm lucky I don't have one of those old plaster casts."

"Well I'm not going sure lucky is the right word because I'm sure you've got plenty of pain, but honestly Daniel, where's your head at these days? A farm can be a very dangerous place if you're not constantly and carefully paying attention."

Samuel speaks up in agreement: "Exactly what I told him Tally. First he cut himself so badly he needed stitches—"

"From Luisa!" chimes in Nora with a chuckle.

"Right, and now these injuries from George. Really, Daniel anyone would think you're accident-prone." Samuel is quite indignant.

"Well distractions do occur..." Miz Tally lets the sentence trail off before changing the subject.

"Milly, you mentioned you had a photo of your parents on their wedding day. I really like pictures like that, can I see it?"

Milly answers *of course* before jumping up to get the framed photo from her bedroom. Of course it's completely familiar but she glances at it with new eyes wondering what Miz Tally will see.

To Milly it's just the hairstyles that show the age because the clothing is well, just the usual wedding wear. Dress whites for her father whose hair is side-parted and slicked down, and a lacy white wedding gown for her mother who sports a beehive hairdo. A mini-dress would better suit that hairstyle from her mother's youth but the bride's dress sweeps the ground and that matches the groom's formal wear.

Naturally everyone wants to have a look at the photo so it gets passed around and squinted at looking for a resemblance.

"Oh how nice! You father was a Naval man and doesn't he look handsome in his uniform?"

"Naval? how can you tell?"

Miz Tally looks from one face to the other before giving her head a slight shake. "You young people... Samuel you at least should know that Army and Air Force formal wear is Dress Blues while Naval men wear white." She tut-tuts before returning her attention to the photo: "Your mother is lovely and looks to be hmm... late thirties, Milly?"

"Possibly even forty or early forties. Again, I've never learned anything directly, not even first-hand gossip, but I remember some talk about a difficult birth that was only to be expected given her age."

"Interesting. Beautiful frame too, it's real silver and by that I mean it's sterling. I can tell by the weight and of course there will be a hallmark as well," her old eyes have no trouble finding the inlaid stamp. "Oh it *is* a Tiffany, I thought it might be... and quite valuable, too."

Esther asks: "How valuable?" and her father gives her a nudge

whispering *Esther, we've talked about this before.*

"I'm sure you could get $5,000. Silver fluctuates but the craftsmanship, the Tiffany name, it might even be worth five times that amount. I think you said your grandmother left you this."

"Yes, that's what I was told."

"I can't imagine what it's like for you Milly, not having any real memories. I mean, my mother passed away too but I don't have to rely on what other people tell me because I remember her. I remember her face and her voice and even her perfume–"

Daniel interrupts Esther saying: "*Lily-of-the-Valley* by Yardley."

Seeing the surprised looks he chuckles saying: "I used to buy it for her for Mother's Day. She told me it was her favorite but I think she chose it because it was relatively inexpensive."

"Oh Daniel, wearing perfume bought by her son would be priceless to any mother," says Miz Tally and Milly feels a pang in her heart at such a touching sentiment.

"Now Milly, this oval frame hides part of the picture which, of course, is square. Your grandmother might have cut the original to fit but I think she'd be more likely to have folded it so may I open up the back and we'll take a look?"

"I never thought of that but sure, so long as it won't tear the photo..."

"Oh I'll be careful, and this frame is so well-made it will open easily."

True to her word the old woman's fingers gently prod the clasps open and the velvety backing and cardboard are pulled away. "Ah yes, it is a studio portrait. The photographer's watermark should be right.. yes, it's here but such a flowery writing I can't quite make it out but hopefully... yes! the name and address is stamped on the back of the photo.

Oh, the ink is quite faded... Esther, your young eyes can see this better than I can so be a dear and read it out loud."

Esther carefully takes hold of the photo and gives out the information: *Philip J. Sinclair Photography Studio, San Diego, California.*

"San Diego makes sense since your father was Navy, Milly," puts in Samuel. "Maybe the reason for their later-in-life marriage was because he was at sea?"

"And she waited for him... oh, how romantic!"

"Now here's a memento that brings back memories," says Miz Tally carefully holding up a dried flower and a strip of yellowing lace. "It was tucked in between the sheets of backing and I suspect it's the corsage your grandmother wore at her daughter's wedding.

Based on your mother's age at the time of her marriage your grandmother would have been my generation so I'm not surprised she kept it, we old ladies can be very sentimental."

"Well it doesn't look like much of anything now," states Esther bluntly and the adults chuckle.

While the photo is gently folded up and everything, including the corsage, put back together again Miz Tally quietly asks Daniel to write down the name of the studio and slip it to her. He discreetly does as she asks marveling to himself at the never-ending curiosity of women.

Less than a week later there's a gathering in the farmhouse's recently cleaned-up front room for a celebration.

"Don't thank me, Milly," says Reverend Smithson. "I helped but truly, this is all down to Miz Tally who figured it all out. She's your Fairy Godmother!"

The Reverend, Miz Tally, and Janice Peart because she invited herself, are congratulating Milly on the discovery of a windfall of money she's entitled to from her parent's estate.

"The Navy takes care of its own Milly, so I knew there must be something from your father. A survivor's benefit or a pension payout, insurance... probably a trust set up in your name, and there was," explains Miz Tally with quiet satisfaction.

Stephen continues the tale saying: "Reverend Johnson put me on to the old lawyer fellow, Ellison, who helped us fill in a few blanks. He'd gotten your Social Security number for you when you applied for this job and it came with your birth certificate both having been registered together as is common in California hospitals.

That plus information from the photographer's records, yes the studio is still operating, gave us a place to start.

Under Miz Tally's direction I did the legwork and we managed to track down someone in Administration who had no difficulty finding the account, and a very respectable sum it is."

Esther opens her mouth to ask *how much?* but closes it when she catches her father's eye on her.

Janice Peart has no such compunction and demands to know: "Just how much is this sum?"

Milly, sifting through the papers in a file folder they've given her, looks up with a stunned expression saying: "Why this is... oh! it's just not possible."

"Of course it is, your parents made arrangements for your care, Milly. Maybe because they were much older than most parents of newborns, or maybe they were just prudent people. They obviously loved you very much."

The young woman, her eyes shining with emotion, reaches out to grasp Miz Tally's hand telling her: "No one's ever said that before. It means a lot, thank you!"

After a moment of everyone enjoying Milly's happiness Stephen picks up the story saying: "The thing is, you slipped through the cracks when your grandmother came to claim you. Probably because it was such a relief to the people in San Diego that you had family to take you in, much better than putting you into the care of the Child Welfare Service."

"Oh that's so true! I've heard terrible things happening from children they'd looked after. But... why did no one tell me about this money?"

"That I'm afraid is typical of the bureaucratic mind-set. The financial service of the Armed Forces never cared what happened to the money, its only concern was to deposit it into the trust fund set up for you. This happened every month until the day you turned eighteen and then it stopped. No questions asked before, during, or at any time after.

Under California law an account with no activity for three years is deemed dormant. If the account owner can't be found any money goes to the State Treasury department. So three years from your eighteenth birthday is your twenty-first, or the day before to be on the safe side, and I think we're just in time!"

"Actually my 21st birthday isn't until next April," Milly says.

"April 1st!" puts in Esther laughing.

Janice Peart exclaims: "On April Fool's Day?"

"Yes, ha-ha I've heard all the jokes because everybody makes fun of me over that."

Miz Tally chides her: "Oh my dear, you're so young! Don't be the butt of the joke instead, make it yours. Say things like *I'm only a fool for one day a year so you've only got today to trick me and you better make it count.*"

"Oh I like that! but I can never think of good comebacks, I'm not that clever."

"No, it's because you're simply too sweet to be snarky. Anyhow, I'm sure we'll need this time because there'll be a process to follow. Your guardian's lawyer, this Matt Ellison, says he's happy to take care of it for you. He told us that Sunshine would be *tickled to bits at the idea of The Man being made to pay.*

Anyhow he'll know all the ins and outs of you being at that foster home–"

"Oh he does. I remember him being angry with Sunshine when he found out my grandmother had literally handed me over without any government involvement or anything like that. Sunshine just snapped at him saying *Good! that's exactly how we want it. The Man doesn't need to be poking his nose into our business.*

He tried to argue asking *but what if the grandmother changes her mind and wants the girl back?* and that's when I learned my grandmother was dead because Sunshine said *No chance of that, the old lady died soon after Milly came to us. Thank goodness, too, because otherwise the child would have been left alone in that house for who knows how long!*"

"Oh I think I would have liked her, she sure sounds like a straight-shooter, a real tough old bird." The words sound funny spoken in Miz Tally's soft-voiced Southern drawl.

"I'm as tough as my feet, she used to say," adds Milly collapsing into a fit of giggles.

"Her feet?"

"Sunshine never wore shoes, it was a thing when she was a young flower-child for the girls to go barefoot. Maybe the boys too, I don't know, but definitely the girls. Well, it sounds all very Mother Nature-y but if you'd seen the state of her feet! Her soles looked like those imported sandals that are probably made out of car tires and cost about a dollar. They were almost black, and hard, and calloused, and the ugliest things you ever saw!"

"Oh but surely she could have had treatment? Did she never see a podiatrist?"

"She said there was no pain from fallen arches or anything because she was naturally flat-footed and she didn't want to *get in the clutches of Big Pharma* as she put it, so no. She truly was just as tough as her feet!"

Janice is determined to bring the conversation back to the point saying: "That's all well and good but let's get back to this money that Milly's getting from the Army."

"Navy," a chorus of voices say in correction.

"It's quite simple, Janice. Milly's father was a Naval man and he'd made provisions when she was born that if anything happened to him she'd inherit via a trust set up until she comes of age."

"Well that seems straightforward so what's all the fuss about?"

"The fuss is because no one knew the trust existed. The grandmother would have known but she died soon after Milly's parents did and there was no one else to share that knowledge."

"Oh now I see! Milly would never have known about this money if you hadn't ferreted it out."

Miz Tally chuckles at her neighbor's choice of words but Milly confirms that Janice is right. "I'd never have thought to go looking because it never occurred to me that there might be any money."

"Nowadays folk take everyone at face value and for the most part I think that's a good thing, we don't want to return to the days of blaming children for *the sins of their fathers*, but in your case my dear nobody thought of you as anything other than *an orphaned child*. I mean, you meant plenty to the people you grew up with but it seems nobody wondered about your antecedents.

Anyone looking at that wedding photo should have realized a Naval man would have had a pension and life insurance at the very least."

"Except for a head-in-the-clouds aging hippie whose inherited wealth meant she never had to think about money, and who lived very frugally regardless."

"Anyhow, it's all being taken care of now and the money will end up in the hands of its rightful owner which is you."

"A real cause for celebration so let's all give a toast to *Milly Moneybags*," teases Samuel and the rest all chime in.

Milly's voice catches as she fervently says: "And all thanks to you, Miz Tally. And you too, Reverend, actually so many people have helped me it's... it's all so nice."

"Yes, but how much money are we talking about?" asks Janice plaintively.

Milly turns to the woman and after taking her time to sort through the papers in her file drops her voice to say: "A lot!"

And the rest of them can't hide their smirks at the sour look of frustration on Janice Peart's face.

The village soon learns about Millie's inheritance. Reaction among the inhabitants varies with the extremes being *doesn't seem right her being a thief and getting rewarded* to, illogically, *that just goes to prove she didn't take that money, she had no need to steal.*

The majority are pleased for Milly who has made a good impression in Sweet Berry Cove. Most figure since the police aren't in any rush to lay charges it's not quite the *open-and-shut case* the gossips claimed it to be.

Daniel has mixed feelings. On the one hand he's happy about Milly's good fortune but on the other, well... what kind of changes will occur now? Surely Milly won't leave, will she? although the last couple of weeks have been difficult for her.

He feels he should have done more to help her. But of course he can't now that he knows about the money because how would that look? Plus everyone knows that large amounts of money often have a curious effect on people and usually not in a positive way.

He can't imagine Milly being the type to let sudden wealth go to her head, she isn't excitable or flighty, but his experience of women has disillusioned him. He doesn't feel he can rely on his own opinion. He really thought, after all the time they'd spent together growing up together, that he knew Helena through and through yet she sure had him fooled.

A Happy Compromise

Esther shifts nervously in one of the visitor chairs in Reverend Smithson's office at the Church. The other chairs are unoccupied because he specifically asked to see her alone. He finishes polishing his glasses and pushes the tissue box across the desk towards her. Esther looks at it with apprehension.

Stephen Smithson knows how to use his voice to best effect and now, as he leans forward, he speaks in a measured tone.

"It's understandable that you're nervous, Esther. This is a very serious situation... very serious indeed. I expect excuses and justifications, possibly lies, definitely tears but we will work together on a resolution. I am on your side Esther, and you have nothing to fear."

Looking into her face he sees the truculence of a moody teen. "Would you like to kick off this discussion with your side of the story?"

Wearing an expression mixed with both guilt and defiance the girl tilts her head to stare behind him at the corner of the room where the wall meets the ceiling. "What's the point? You've already made up your mind."

"Oh I have, yes," he readily agrees before continuing: "But there is an alternative solution... something that was actually put forward by Milly Clarke herself."

He notes how Esther's mouth twists in a petulant pout at mention of Milly and has to tamp down the sudden flare of anger he feels.

"Esther, Milly Clarke is the wronged party here. For many weeks she has been subjected to cruel and vile behavior because you let the villagers believe she stole money."

"I never said a word against her!"

"You deliberately withheld the truth that would have exonerated her and you did so with malice aforethought."

Stephen's voice deepens as he outlines the effects of Esther's transgression.

"You are guilty of sinning, Esther. A sin of omission is no less evil than a sin of commission.

You not only hid the facts you did so knowing full well what the repercussions would be. Gossip, slander, whispering, and finger-pointing."

As his words hit home Esther finds her eyes have returned to meet his and now she can't tear her gaze away. She's blinking back tears and worrying a hangnail as she sinks deeper into her chair, shoulders hunched and slumping.

Reverend Smithson is relentless.

"Milly proposed that the family should lie to save you from any unpleasantness." He sees how the girl perks up in hope at this idea and feels a grim satisfaction in quashing it.

"When your father came to me about it I strongly advised against this course of action. As he knew I would because it's wrong. Lying is wrong, hiding from consequences is also wrong, and running away from the ugly truth about ourselves is wrong, wrong, wrong."

"Bu-but what is this story? What could we say?"

"The suggested story does hang together, it's plausible, but once the made-up tale is spread around well... you know what people will say, right? They'll say that this reeks of a cover-up – which is completely true – and then that poisonous old saw of *there's no smoke without fire.* That innocent young woman's reputation and good name will languish because of your sin."

"I can't help what other people say!" the girl bursts out, "It's not my fault if they want to talk and spread lies–"

"But it is your fault, Esther. It's 100% your fault."

"No, I never made any accusations, I never said a word against Milly, I–"

"You made your so-called discovery of the theft when you opened the safe in front of witnesses that morning, correct?"

"Uh, yes, there were um.. people there."

Speaking slowly and clearly Reverend Smithson asks: "Why did you open the safe?"

Esther stares at him open-mouthed and wide-eyed. The color drains from her face when she realizes he's figured out that she engineered it all. Still, she tries to bluster saying: "What do you mean? We use the safe every day."

"Every day that the Young Family's Farm Shop is open for business and making sales then yes, you do. You open the safe at the end of the day to put away the money and receipts but that wasn't the case at all, was it? You had no need to open the safe that morning except to expose it's emptiness in front of witnesses."

Straining forward in her desperation to deflect blame Esther practically shouts: "I never knew that Janice Peart would call the police in!"

"No, I'm sure you found that turn of events quite frightening–"

"Oh I did, I was terrified!"

"Then imagine that terror magnified ten-fold and you'll have an idea of what Milly Clarke felt."

Esther can't hold back her sobs a moment longer. She's struggled with sham indignation and disdain but the reverend's accusations have stripped away layer after layer until she just feels cold inside.

Pushing down his pity for the girl Stephen continues with his questions: "How can you remove the stain of sin from your soul if you don't confess, Esther?"

Lifting her tear-streaked face to him Esther cries out: "Oh I do confess, Reverend. I do. I didn't tell the truth and... and I did... uh, plan for Milly to get blamed."

"Why?"

"Oh! I don't know... I don't... um, well she and Nora spent all their time together laughing and talking and... and everybody likes her! You like her."

"I do. I think she's an exceptionally nice young lady. She's personable and pretty, friendly and helpful and respectful. Whatever did she do to you to deserve this?"

Sullen again Esther has to admit Milly has done nothing against her.

"In fact, she's treated you with kindness and courtesy, right?"

Her face crumpling again in tears Esther just nods.

"So Milly deserves your apology?"

Taking a deep breath Esther swallows before agreeing: "Yes, yes I do owe her an apology."

"In public."

"What?"

"You harmed her in public so you must make amends in public."

Getting up from his chair Stephen comes around to sit on the edge of his desk and take hold of Esther's hands. His compassion shows in his posture, his words, and the gentle expression on his face.

"I will help you, Esther. At church this Sunday I will explain that the money was never missing after all, that your brother Amos who had every right to take it did so and you can confirm this because you were there. I would like you to stand up then and turn to face the congregation as you say: *I give Milly Clarke my heartfelt apology for what she went through. I got scared when I saw how everybody acted and I was afraid to tell the truth.* And then sit down and I'll thank you for clearing it up.

No questions, no conversation, just a teenage girl being brave and doing the right thing, and sharing out the blame for the bad behavior of grown-ups who should have known better."

"I-I don't think I can..."

Bestowing a genuine smile on her Stephen says: "Esther Young, I *know* you can."

It's a very subdued Esther who sits down at the dinner table on that Saturday night. Samuel already gave a heads-up to the household not to inquire about Esther's meeting with Stephen, at the Reverend Smithson's request. In confidence he told his good friend Samuel that he doesn't want Esther dramatizing herself because of getting too much attention.

It's lucky Esther won't have too long to fret over her upcoming ordeal in the church but nevertheless she's certain to have an anxious sleepless night.

Next morning Reverend Smithson times his introduction to Esther perfectly: not too early so the congregation won't whisper and speculate throughout the service, but not so late that Esther makes herself sick with nerves.

The girl performs her part exactly right, her one verbal stumble adding sincerity to the words, and after his closing remarks the reverend starts them off singing an uplifting and joyous hymn.

People notice how Milly's talented voice sings out strong and steady. Daniel's baritone is missed but he's at home resting his ankle. Although he's well on the way to recovery he didn't mind skipping this morning's service.

The family return home full of praise for Esther giving her public apology and both Samuel and Daniel regret missing it. Esther happily repeats her performance for them, having memorized the words *just like lines for the school play* she explains.

"So Milly what were your lines in this bit of play-acting?" asks Daniel with an amused glint in his eye.

"Me? Nobody told me what was going to happen so I just sat there with my mouth hanging open and looking incredibly foolish, I'm sure."

"Not at all!" exclaims Nora. "You smiled graciously and gave Esther's hand a squeeze. Everyone saw."

"I guess that's a happy compromise but I'm not sure if you're treating it in the spirit Stephen intended–" begins Samuel, but his eldest interrupts to say that *Esther did a bang-up job and that should put a stop to the talk once and for all.*

Hannah laughs the loudest when Amos says that knowing full well this tale will become village lore that's discussed for years to come.

All's Fair in Love and War

While his ankle recovers Daniel and Bernie spend their days at the Young Family's Farm Shop with Milly. Daniel helps with the bookkeeping for the online store while Milly preps her orders.

They work well together, neither feeling any constraint, and the two of them talk about everything under the sun. Currently they're planning out Milly's brainstorm of having a small counter-service cafe.

"When we first talked about this with Dad I think you mentioned something small and casual?"

"Exactly, just a few chairs around a couple of tables, and no Wi-Fi! we don't want them to plug in and hang out all day."

"Sweet Berry Cove doesn't really go for hang-outs, no one has that kind of time actually–"

"Teenagers do."

"Nope, not even them. It's *all hands on deck* so to speak when it comes to running a family farm."

"So you don't think there's a market for this idea?"

"Oh I know there is. With all the seasonal treats you're making and selling the Farm Shop will become a regular stopover for shoppers. The idea of sitting for a snack and a chinwag after they've studied the latest offerings will be irresistible. You'll be a hit, Milly. No doubt about it."

"Oh good! The pumpkin spice has gone over really well because all the big coffee chains have already done the marketing, whetting everyone's appetite. Ooh! that was a pun!" she giggles.

"You just have to figure out how much you're going to charge."

Milly explains with great enthusiasm that she's already worked out a menu of so much for a slice of pie, a piece of cake, a square, and every purchase will include a free coffee. The only choice will be regular or decaf, so no special machines required or fancy barista skills.

"Will people mind not having ice cream with their pie? I mean we can provide it, but if we do I'll need a freezer. Oh and also a dishwasher for the coffee mugs. I'll need plates and cutlery, too." At her frown Daniel tells her not to worry, the Farm Shop will cover the initial outlay.

"Who knows? Maybe someday you'll be running a catering firm out of here."

"Oh Daniel! that sounds... but no, I don't want to spend every waking minute working, that's too much pressure. I want to always enjoy doing my job."

An incident that occurred shortly after they re-opened the Farm Shop brought the two of them closer and their friendship has deepened every day since.

Helena, Daniel's erstwhile *fiancee* came by. She's been back in the village for a while now but no one knows if she's still visiting or if she and her husband have called it quits.

Ostensibly she's come by to commiserate with Daniel and cheer on his recovery, but it quickly becomes clear her main interest is Milly's inheritance.

After the introductions and a perfunctory *how're you getting on then?* to Daniel she leans on the counter and begins quizzing Milly about when will she get her money? where is she planning to go? what will she be investing in? what will her first big purchase be? until Milly, laughing, puts up her hand and says: "Stop!"

"I'm not going anywhere, I love it here in Sweet Berry Cove. It's a beautiful place to call home."

"Here? Seriously? There's nothing to do! There are no shops, no entertainment, no culture!"

"There's fresh air, luscious fruit, wide-open spaces, a beautiful landscape and seascape, and the leisure to enjoy it all. And I haven't even gotten to all the great friends I've made. I have no interest in moving away. As for my first big purchase well I have two things in mind–"

"Oooh, what are you getting yourself?"

"For me, a car. I've already saved up about half the cost of nice little used car but who knows? maybe I'll let the salesman talk me into a new model."

Helena's smile is more of a grimace, she's clearly unimpressed with Milly's aspirations. "What's the second thing?"

"Oh that's something I am excited about, I'm going to get a proper headstone for Sunshine's grave. Sunshine was my *de facto* guardian and a wonderful, wonderful person. She's buried in the Calvary churchyard back home along with some famous people and she deserves to be honored. I'm proud to do something fitting for her."

Daniel joins the conversation asking: "Won't her heirs take care of that, Milly?"

"No, they never even met her. They'll just instruct their lawyer to order the legal minimum from the funeral home. No, it's my privilege to do this."

The warmth of the smile Daniel gives spreads right through her.

Impatiently Helena interrupts their silent communing to ask: "But what about the rest? I heard you're getting lots and lots of money, so what are you going to do with it?"

The woman's eyes shine with greed and the disdainful looks she's been casting over Milly betray her envy.

"Oh that's easy, the bulk of my money will go into long-term savings for the education of the children I hope to have some day."

Just as Helena grimaces Daniel applauds Milly's choice. "That's an excellent idea. Not everyone wants to farm and the world needs doctors and lawyers too."

"Oh they don't have to become professionals, I would never impose any condition except one: they must do what makes them happy. That might be becoming a CPA or throwing clay on a potter's wheel or raising fruit on a family farm. The money will assist them to achieve their heart's desire."

Daniel finds himself nodding his happy agreement at this long-range plan. Milly's head isn't being turned by her new-found wealth, she's just as sensible and down-to-earth as ever, she'll never feel the need to lord it over anyone. Her words are heart-felt and prove that she wants to stay at the farm and she wants to marry and raise a family.

Dissatisfied and disappointed Helena takes her leave soon afterwards.

"Daniel, do you think this means she no longer wants to be my new BFF?"

He laughs loudly at her wisecrack, bestowing such a wide grin on her that Milly feels deep-down that she's already found her BFF and he's right here.

At closing Amos shows up in the *Gator* to drive Daniel back to the farmhouse. It's a handy little vehicle that Milly said *looks like a fancy golf-cart* but the brothers hastened to explain that this *farm utility vehicle* is so much more.

Every day they offer Milly a lift back but it would mean sitting on Daniel's lap so she refuses.

"That couldn't possible do his ankle the least bit of good so thanks but no thanks, I'll walk."

"I don't know Milly, having you cuddled on his lap would be a heck of a distraction from any pain..." teases Amos, waggling his eyebrows.

Milly darts a quick glance at the younger brother expecting to see his familiar scowl but instead he's rolling his eyes with a hint of a smile quirking one corner of his mouth. When he catches her eye his lips flatten into no expression which is still better than usual.

"Tempting as that sounds," she replies in a sarcastic tone, "I'll have to pass. I spend my days taste-testing home-baked cakes and pies so I need all the exercise I can get, otherwise..."

If she's fishing for a compliment she's successful in the admiring onceovers each of the men give her, but neither is rude enough to ogle or stare. "Besides, walking my pathway is quicker than your drive down the lane."

"This little beauty can easily navigate that path, or no path even, but I better not jostle the invalid over bumpy terrain."

"Look Amos, I walk here to the Farm Shop every morning. I don't need a ride home, walking is good for me," retorts Daniel turning to look his brother in the eye.

"After being up all day, even if you are mostly sitting, your ankle needs rest not more exercise. Are we gonna have this argument every night?"

"Not if I can help it. Doc Watkins is coming to check me over tomorrow and I'll ask him point-blank." More to himself than conversationally Daniel adds:

"That reminds me... I need to ask him about something else, too. He probably thinks I forgot or was delirious from the pain or something but I heard his snide *consult with Luisa* remark."

Dismissing his brother's muttering Amos pointedly ignores Daniel and calls out: "Okay Milly, the ingrate and I will see you back at the farmhouse," and the two of them drive away.

Bernie gallops alongside the vehicle for a bit before cutting through the field to catch up with Milly. Because of the dog's frequent stops to sniff she's dawdling on her return trip and arrives just before the men do.

After waiting patiently a moment while Daniel struggles to get out of the *Gator* Milly steps forward to assist him up the stairs to the porch.

He sighs but allows his arm to be taken without saying a word. This is a great improvement over the continual argument that ended only recently. Daniel hates to be reliant on anyone and it seems especially so with Milly. She doesn't speak either as she lends her support to get him up each step.

Milly is very aware of Daniel's smell, a cedar body-wash mixed with his natural male scent, and the warmth of him emanating through his flannel shirt. Daniel is silently admitting to himself how relaxing he finds the closeness of this placid young woman with her lavender-scented hair and a surprisingly strong grip in her small hands.

Amos left to put the vehicle away but now that he's returned Milly steps free of Daniel and turning, looks up into his face to see that he's steadied himself and is okay.

Amos sees that tonight's setting sun, a particularly deep orange color, is spreading its glow and catching their eyes in a bronze light. Both Milly and Daniel seems suspended as if time has paused for the long moment they spend wordlessly gazing at each other.

The sound of Amos's foot on the stair frees them from the temporary spell but it's a slow awakening. Neither of them startle. Milly says *I'll see you at dinner* in a quiet but steady voice while Daniel's tone is thoughtful as he confirms this.

The two men watch her turn and make her way inside. She carefully holds the screen-door to prevent its usual clattering close. After at least a minute's silence Amos comments: "I think you're falling in love, bro."

Nora is coming down the stairs to meet up with husband, hoping they can enjoy some time sitting on the porch swing. She freezes hearing his words. Putting a finger to her lips for quiet she grabs Milly's hand dragging her back down the stairs and forcing the younger woman to eavesdrop with her.

Milly is reluctant, not wanting to hear out loud the words she already knows.

"Oh I fell a while ago," replies Daniel ruefully.

Milly's mouth falls open and her face takes on a look of wonder.

"I just don't know how to make up for the way I treated her before, especially after well... you know. I mean, I never came out and accused her of stealing but neither did I say I believed her."

The men aren't speaking loudly but their deep voices, so similiar, carry on the still night. Inside the two women exchange round-eyed looks of surprise.

Shaking his head Amos again apologizes saying: "I am so sorry for all the trouble I caused when–"

"Amos, seriously, you did nothing wrong. It just turned into a weird thing that snowballed and you know, a lot of honesty came out of that, I mean... the way people acted was a real surprise, both good and bad, and well, it's always best to know where everyone stands when things get rough."

"So what are you going to do now?"

"I don't know Amos, I just don't know," Daniel pauses a moment, a confused look on his face. "What would you do?"

"Me? I'd grovel. You know: roses, jewelry, chocolates, romantic dates, begging... somehow I can't see you doing any of those things, though. You're more of a big gesture kind of guy."

"Well... I did save her from drowning so that was kind of big."

Amos is really surprised and practically shouts his questions: "When? What happened? Why has nobody said anything?"

Nora tilts her head in a silent question and Milly nods furiously. This shakes her out of the shocked state Daniel's declaration has brought. Now she listens eagerly.

Thinking back to the events of that afternoon Daniel slowly answers: "I don't think anyone other than Dad and Hannah ever knew, not at the time at least, and I can't imagine who Milly would have spoken to about it afterwards. I certainly didn't say anything to anyone."

"She owes you her life! Milly just needs reminding of that with reinforcement from the rest of us. I'll introduce the subject of um, drowning or swimming or something, no wait, I'll mention that you're a strong swimmer and ask if you've ever had to come to someone's aid in the water. Oh, this is perfect Dan. If you rescued Milly from drowning then you really are a hero, her hero!"

"I don't know, Amos. It all seems... well, like play-acting and that's Esther's department, I don't think I could carry it off. It would be too fake, contrived–"

"Hey, you know what they say *all's fair in love and war.*"

There's a lengthy pause while Daniel is considering the idea. Finally he says: "Don't say anything yet, I want to sleep on it. I don't think I'll be up long after dinner tonight."

"Okay but... I can't believe the drowning story never made the rounds. I mean, everybody knows everyone's business here in Sweet Berry Cove. I can't tell you how many people have told me about Milly taking you to the vet to get sewn up. Anyhow, let's go in."

There's a sudden panicked flurry inside as Milly tries to push past Nora who is stifling a laugh at her friend's antics.

Nora loudly stomps on the stairs calling: "Amos? Is that you out on the porch?" Just before opening the door. She can hear Milly still scampering up behind her so she acts clumsy, blocking Daniel's entrance for a minute before the two of them laugh and she steps aside ushering him in.

"I'm coming in too, sweetheart," says Amos.

Taking him by the arm Nora explains *I thought we could sit outside for a bit since it's a cold supper so no rush to go eat. Besides, it's actually quite a pleasant night, not chilly at all.*

Amos loves the idea and before he even seats his bride on the porch swing he steals a kiss.

Although it's not late farm life starts early so it's not long after that both Daniel and Milly are in their respective beds. Neither one is able to sleep right away, both of them having too much to think about.

Daniel wonders if he can somehow use his saving of Milly's life as a way to capture her heart. He doesn't realize he already has. Milly is also trying to think of a solution for him without giving away what she overheard.

They both fall asleep about an hour later. Daniel still hasn't figured it out, but Milly has already formulated a plan.

After the breakfast has been eaten and everything tidied away Milly and Daniel set out for their slow walk to the Farm Shop. It will warm up later on, after an afternoon's worth of sunshine, but it's still cool enough for jackets mid-morning.

All of the household members have taken to carrying dog treats in their jacket pockets but today Milly has secreted a hunk of cheddar cheese. Bernie keeps butting her with his head, bestowing lots of licks, and generally sticking to her side like a burr.

When the dog suddenly moves in front causing her to almost stumble Daniel, exasperated, exclaims: "What is wrong with Bernie today?"

"Oh he's feeling remorseful and I'm afraid that's my fault," Milly replies.

"Remorseful? huh! that dog doesn't have a conscience."

"Yes he does, don't you boy?" croons Milly scratching Bernie's ears. He likes the petting but is far more interested in finding the cheese he can maddeningly smell.

Lightly laughing Daniel says: "Okay, I'll bite, why is Bernie remorseful?"

Turning to him with her eyes blinking wide Milly answers: "Because he almost got me killed! Daniel I would have drowned if it wasn't for you and it's all because of Bernie getting himself out on that rock and pretending he was trapped there."

The previous night's conversation coming to mind leaves Daniel speechless over the coincidence of Milly bringing up the very subject!

"So now he's very sorry about scaring me like that, right Bernie?" The dog jumps up trying to lick Milly's face.

"In fact," she continues as her lips helplessly twitch into a smile, "Remembering and talking about it made me feel so faint Bernie suggested maybe you should *check my temperature* again."

Stopping, Daniel studies first Bernie then Milly and his suspicions are confirmed watching the latter struggling to hide her smile. Looking at her properly his expression turns serious although a slight smile tugs at the corner of his mouth.

Lifting one eyebrow Daniel draws Milly towards him possessively and tilting up her face murmurs *that Bernie is a clever puppy* before giving her her first kiss ever... and it's the warmest, sweetest, longest kiss she could hope for.

The emotion, the surety, the love, conveyed in that tender kiss speaks to Milly's soul. Their second kiss makes her toes curl.

Pulled tight into Daniel's embrace she knows there's no where else she will ever want to be except here with him. Milly has found her forever home in Daniel's arms, and both of them have discovered their life-long loves in Sweet Berry Cove.

And they all lived happily ever after.

FINDING LOVE IN SWEET BERRY COVE

Dear Reader:

Thank you so much for choosing *"Finding Love in Sweet Berry Cove"*, and I hope you enjoyed it!

Please consider leaving a review. Reviews help make books discoverable by other readers, and help authors in rankings.

In grateful appreciation,

Ness Woodberry

www.ingramcontent.com/pod-product-compliance
Lightning Source LLC
Chambersburg PA
CBHW031948240626
47153CB00003B/901